MURDER
AT
ELAINE'S

MURDER AT ELAINE'S

A NOVEL BY
RON ROSENBAUM

STONEHILL

*I'd like to thank Tom Forcade for offering me the challenge of
writing an old-fashioned mystery serial in his magazine,* High
Times, *and for his inspired editorial suggestions. Thanks, also, to
Susan Wyler and Shelly Levitt of the magazine for editorial aid
and comfort during the monthly deadline crises; Pat Berens for her
encouragement; Michael Drosnin for his friendship and advice;
and to Doug Taylor and Michael Doret whose illustrations cap-
tured that mystery serial flavor so well and made the project as
fun to look at as it was to write. And, special thanks, to Caroline
Marshall for everything.*

Portions of MURDER AT ELAINE'S originally appeared, in somewhat
different form, in *High Times Magazine,* for whose cooperation,
the Publishers would like to express their appreciation.

ISBN: 0-88373-083-9
LIBRARY OF CONGRESS CATALOG CARD NUMBER 78-64635

Illustrations and special type design by Doug Taylor and
Michael Doret.

First Printing

Printed in the USA

For Henry, Evelyn and Ruth

T A B L E   O F   C O N T E N T S

Prologue:

The Apartment, A True Story

It is generally agreed among aficionados of the arcana of Watergate that, of all the elaborate schemes dreamed up by the Plumbers and other shady secret operatives of the Nixon administration, none was more demented, none more depraved than the one that came to be known as the "Golden Greek Affair."

This bizarre plot, hatched in the summer of '71, grew out of the Nixon operatives' obsession with the threat of a Teddy Kennedy presidential candidacy in 1972; its ultimate objective was discovery of the Secret Story of Chappaquiddick.

The Nixon operatives believed in the notion of the Secret Story with a grail-like devotion: they were sure that somewhere, somehow, there was someone who would tell them what *really* happened to Kennedy and Kopechne that night, and that it would turn out to be something so dark and scandalous that, when revealed, would exorcise the Nixon Presidency of Kennedy ghosts forever.

The moment they learned about the death of Mary Jo Kopechne, the Nixon "offensive intelligence" specialists were convinced that the pro-Kennedy clique in the media would let their fair-haired favorite off the hook—and that they would have to do some "investigative reporting" of their own.

Depositions on file with the Senate Special Watergate Committee tell of Bebe Rebozo and John Ehrlichman watching the network reports of Chappaquiddick on a TV set at the Key Biscayne White House. The two discussed the need to ensure that Teddy Kennedy didn't escape tough questions about his role in the tragedy. Action followed: Runyonesque ex-cop and private eye Tony Ulasciewicz was dispatched to Chappaquiddick to pose as a reporter and ask embarrassing questions. White House people had quite a chuckle later at seeing their man at televised press conferences making the Kennedy spokesmen squirm. But aside from chuckles, Ulasciewicz failed to find the One True Secret.

The operatives didn't give up: they tracked down every lead. When they heard a rumor that a certain party in Providence, Rhode Island, a one-time night manager of a hotel on Martha's Vineyard, across from Chappaquiddick, was in possession of some explosive information, E. Howard Hunt himself was dispatched on a mission to Providence—equipped with a CIA device to disguise his voice and other inept tools of deception—to pry the secret from this person. But even Hunt, who had fabricated a JFK cable ordering the assassination of Diem, failed to find even the most threadbare material in this Providence "source" with which to fabricate a Secret Story.

Next, they tried direct surveillance of Senator Kennedy: operatives were dispatched to his hotel in Hawaii during a Senate junket to see if they could snoop out something scandalous enough to revive the taint of Chappaquiddick. Nothing.

Time was running out. Rumors of a Kennedy candidacy continued to mount. Columnists began to speculate that the public had forgiven Teddy and talked about a Nixon-Kennedy rerun in '72. Nixon's agents knew that nothing would gall the Boss more than the idea of losing again to a Kennedy. To derail his candidacy before he announced, to destroy it by discovering the Secret Story—for this particular project the sky would be the limit: no dirty trick would be too dirty, so long as it worked.

They had shown themselves ready to use blackmail in the plot to steal Dark Secrets from Daniel Ellsberg's shrink. They had shown themselves ready to use drugs to dose Jack Anderson with LSD. They had shown themselves ready to use sex in the "hookers in the houseboats" scheme proposed by G. Gordon Liddy as a blackmail weapon against Democratic delegates to the Miami convention.

In the Golden Greek scheme, they showed themselves prepared to combine *all* these noxious elements in a plan more ludicrous and degrading than any previous ones. Had it been executed, it would have been the dirtiest of all dirty tricks. That it was even *conceived* may alone qualify it for that perverse tribute.

In essence, the President's Men decided they had to abandon the passive and peripheral search for the One True Secret. They devised a more insidious and intimate route to the "truth": they would blackmail the Boiler Room Girls.

The Boiler Room Girls. They were the five women (including Mary Jo Kopechne) who attended the Chappaquiddick clambake that day in July, 1969. During Bobby Kennedy's short-lived Presidential campaign, they had worked the telephone in the feverish delegate hunting headquarters dubbed the Boiler

Room. After the assassination, they had stayed close to the Kennedy family; the Chappaquiddick picnic was to be a celebration and a memorial to the tragedy that had united their lives.

During the inquests and the sensational controversy that followed the death of Mary Jo Kopechne, the Boiler Room Girls lived up to their collective nickname. They took the heat and pressure without a leak. In their testimony, all the Boiler Room Girls supported the essence of Teddy Kennedy's version of his movements on the fatal night. And in the weeks and months that followed, they all consistently refused to say a single word more on the matter to anyone.

The Golden Greek operation was aimed at breaking that silence. The idea was to begin by bugging the apartments of the Boiler Room Girls, probing into their private lives to discover which of them would be most vulnerable.

Enter the man known as the Golden Greek. He was said to be a friend of Liddy or Caulfield, an ex-cop with a reputation as a ladies' man who earned his nickname from his supposed Adonis-like appearance.

He was established in residence in a luxury apartment on Manhattan's Upper East Side. In addition to plush furnishing, the Greek's trysting place was especially equipped with an elaborate videotaping system discreetly concealed behind screens and one-way mirrors. With the help of their friends in the intelligence community (both the CIA and the DEA are reported to use such "honey traps" to compromise and blackmail diplomatic targets) the Nixon men would create the most sophisticated electronic love nest money could buy.

They would survey the habits of the target women by finding their favorite haunts, and then let loose the Golden Greek. His mission: to meet them, chat them up, eventually bring them back to his wired pad. There he was to seduce them with the cameras rolling—slip them psychedelic drugs if necessary to liven up the proceedings. If his charm failed to induce them voluntarily to murmur Chappaquiddick memories as part of their pillow talk, the rough stuff would begin. Extortion.

The Boiler Room Girls would receive photographs of themselves in drug-induced transports of passion. Recipients of the pictures would be informed that those parties, in possession of the full tapes from which the sordid stills had been culled, would assure the wide and embarrassing circulation of the intimate photographs if they didn't comply with certain requests.

They would be asked to attend a private conference. They would be asked certain questions; veracity of the answers might be checked by means of sodium pentothal or a polygraph machine. They might be asked to sign a statement. If there were no real "secret of Chappaquiddick" buried somewhere in their brains, a sordid fiction might be forcefully manufactured.

Such were the mad pornographic workings of the minds of the "offensive intelligence" agents.

How far did they actually go with the scheme?

The phones of two of the Boiler Room Girls *were* tampered with during the summer of 1971. An expensive Upper East Side apartment was rented and furnished by Caulfield and his boys that summer. On a trip to New York, John Dean described visiting the love nest they had prepared. He had been given a key to the place by Caulfield to use for a weekend date, presumably at a time the Greek was out of town. The place had been built up to Dean as a super-sophisticated seduction pad, and so the President's counsel was shocked when he walked into the apartment and found the place covered with tacky pink shag rugs and gilt mirrors, red-and-black leather furniture, and other garish but expensive fixtures. It looked "like some fancy Chicago whorehouse," Dean remarked. Apparently this was the Greek's or the Nixon men's idea of how to impress girls. But Dean's account fails to answer the question: Was it put to use?

At this point, conjecture must replace depositions. Many questions about the ultimate outcome of the Golden Greek operation have not been resolved. With its mandate and budget running out, investigators for the Senate Watergate Committee could not spend the time required to track down every lead in what was considered at the time a bizarre and disgusting, but peripheral, issue to the central question of "what the

President knew and when he knew it." Sources inside the Ervin committee leaked some details of the plot to Woodward and Bernstein, who first made it public in the *Washington Post* of August 1, 1973. But the revelation came at a time when the disclosure of the White House taping system dominated the news. Few reporters followed up the story, and it disappeared from the press.

Nor did the House Impeachment Committee devote any time to exploring the Golden Greek operation; it did not promise to become the "smoking gun"—that dramatic bit of evidence they were so frantically looking for. And after the smoking-gun tape finally drove the President out of office, the official investigating bodies closed their books on the unanswered questions about such lesser dirty tricks that littered their files.

What actually happened to the elaborate electronic honey trap after the summer of 1971? Was it ever used? Some investigators assumed that the apartment operation was made moot after Teddy Kennedy abruptly announced his withdrawal from presidential consideration in the fall of that year. Others speculated that the project was abandoned when the Greek repeatedly struck out in his attempts to get a date with any of the target women, and that the Washington-based faction of the offensive intelligence operation cut the budget out from under the New York faction's pet project.

Other investigators suggested the possibility that the place *was* put to use, that the Washington-based faction may have taken over the operation for their own purposes. The Enemies List had more than just Kennedy's name on it. The trysting place of the Golden Greek may not have been a smoking gun; it was a time bomb.

I

THE NIGHT THE LIGHTS WENT OUT

Sometime around 3:00 A.M. that steamy August night, Princess Rizzoli's chauffeur, Anthony, decided he just had to light up a joint. This waiting around got on his nerves. Since midnight he'd been sitting idle behind the wheel of the Princess' Rolls-Royce Silver Cloud sedan double-parked outside of Elaine's restaurant, the big-shot literary celebrity hangout.

"Keep the engine running," the Princess had trilled out to him as she and her companions bounced out of the back seat. "We're just going to dash in and wave to some friends."

Fat chance, thought Anthony. He'd been through this dozens of times. The Princess and her jet-set companions—tonight they were a once-talented alcoholic playwright and the hot young Brazilian plastic surgeon who was in New York, the official story went, to raise funds for a charity clinic—would all emerge giggling at 4:00 A.M. closing time with some loud-mouth media fat cat.

Anthony was used to this, but the waiting wouldn't have gotten on his nerves if the Princess hadn't been strictly opposed to his smoking dope in her car. It made her bodyguards nervous, the Princess said.

So not long after 3:00 A.M. Anthony decided to risk sneaking off to the phone booth on the corner for a few clandestine puffs. Stepping out of the climate-controlled Cloud onto the sidewalk in front of the entrance to Elaine's was like stepping into a stale sauna.

Hours of idling had turned the limo grilles into massive hotplates blasting the air with withering gusts of engine heat. By the time the chauffeur finally reached the phone booth he was sweating profusely under his black uniform and peaked cap.

He couldn't help wondering a little at the sheer quantity of VIP limos here tonight. Strange, he thought, picking his way through shoals of Clouds, Continentals, and SL 290's to reach the curb, strange that tonight, a dead night in a dead month, these people would all choose to show up and stay till closing time. He recognized the drivers from other late-night vigils outside Elaine's. This guy drove a network anchorman he loved; that guy drove the head of a publishing empire he hated; another guy freelanced for Paramount big shots—even celebrities among limo drivers were here tonight. Inside the booth, as he lit up, Anthony noticed a gleaming dark-green Bentley glide down Second Avenue past Elaine's, turn right at 88th Street and halt halfway down the block behind him.

Still arriving, Anthony thought to himself as he turned back to gaze at the awning over the entrance to Elaine's and the limos flocking around it. Weird, he thought. No one's leaving. Usually they don't all stay to the last minute of closing time. But it struck him that he hadn't seen anyone leave the place for some time.

Why do they do it? he wondered as he lit up and sucked in the pollen-heavy Santa Marta gold. Why are the Princess and her jet-set pals so obsessed with this Elaine's place? They could be anywhere in the world. Why tonight did they have to be here? It must be like a drug for them, whatever it was inside the place, he figured. A powerful drug.

Inside Elaine's, all was cool, sweet, and subtly incandescent as the night waned toward closing time.

Candle flames flickered over the blue-checked table-cloths, guttered to the bottoms of their glasses, flared up and gleamed on the book jackets set into the dark wood-paneled walls. Conversations, too, guttered and flared fitfully at the crowded tables, and flushed faces leaned toward each other over the dregs of drinks studded with stubbed-out cigarette butts. No one got up to leave, even after the bartender announced "Last call."

Elaine, herself, owner of the place and unchallenged arbiter of status in the literary celebrity world that swirled about her, is sitting at her post at the end of the bar, playing backgammon with one of the bartenders, occasionally looking up to sip a seltzer and survey the scene.

Sitting on a bar stool behind Elaine, a slim young man in a black dinner jacket and bowtie sips a Pernod and looks up to survey Elaine. Stuart St. George, an unofficial stringer for the "Suzy Says" society and celebrity column, was, as usual, trying to analyze the patroness' mood this evening.

St. George had higher ambitions for the many nights he spent at Elaine's than mere gossip-column items. Some day, he dreamed, he would write the authorized biography of Elaine and her salon, some day, that is, when she'd finally deign to speak to him and recognize the unique sensibility and devotion to this subject matter that he could bring.

Quite simply, St. George was infatuated with

Elaine, with the Olympian assemblage of brilliant, talented, and famous people who had become devotees of the scene there, with the whole idea of Elaine's, this fabulous "House of Fame"—as he was planning to entitle his bio—a reference to the curious and incomplete fourteenth-century epic poem of Chaucer called "The House of Fame." Yes, thought St. George with some satisfaction, he liked that literary reference. What depth and sensitivity he could bring to this deceptively shallow subject! He knew exactly how he'd begin. St. George smiled inwardly with pleasure at the aptness of his proposed opening epigraph, a quotation from Chaucer scholar E. Talbot Donaldson's commentary on "The House of Fame":

> The Temple of Fame is a very ornate structure filled with the statues of all the famous poets and historians of the past. There, the goddess is enthroned and men appear before her to establish their claim in regard to fame. The goddess' dispositions are wildly whimsical. Some who have deserved and desire good fame are granted it; others equally worthy are given ill fame; others receive oblivion. Some who have deserved ill fame receive good fame. Throughout, the goddess maintains an attitude of righteous virtue, regardless of how wrong her judgements may be.

Exactly, thought St. George. Elaine's restaurant was America's House of Fame and Elaine herself its goddess, dispensing the favor of a precious place at a front table with the righteous and whimsical authority of Chaucer's Goddess of Fame.

St. George could never forget that first moment he knew this celebrated little place, this tight little island of literary celebrity, this Elaine's, would become the center of his life, his work, his destiny. It was August, 1975, and he had just graduated from Princeton when he had come upon an amazing article in *New York* magazine. He could still recall passages of it word for word. Ostensibly, it was a battlefront report on "the great saloon war" of that summer: a one-time waiter at Elaine's named Nicola had opened his own restaurant nearby and was making a flashy but short-lived challenge to Elaine's for the patronage of lit-crowd celebrities' status-conscious Beautiful People that summer. What St. George adored about the article was not so much the mock-heroic reports of the feud, but the delicious little asides dropped into the story by writer Gael Greene, along with the names. The attitudes, the anecdotes, all told with the tongue-in-cheek authority of an Elaine's insider, enchanted St. George.

He recalled Greene's description of the rise of Elaine's: "It began years ago in an unabashedly seedy neighborhood bar at 1703 Second Avenue near 88th Street." Then, slowly, it became a literary hangout as Nelson Aldrich, George Plimpton and the genteel but fashionable *Paris Review* crowd became regulars. Then came Jack Richardson and "a drift of lean, off-

Broadway playwrights," as Gael Greene put it. The place became a nighttime home away from home for some of the most talented new journalists and writers in the mid-Sixties. "That was about the time journalists came to be seen as sexy," Gael Greene quoted David Halberstam, author of *The Best and the Brightest,* a towering figure at the front tables of Elaine's.

Soon, the fashionable world was flocking to Elaine's to see and be seen among the new literary sex objects. *Vogue* and *Harper's Bazaar* did stories on the fashionable fusion of the elites at Elaine's, where Elaine served as "the Earth Mother, nursing them along, trading gossip, taking confessions."

Women's Wear "found the Elaine's mix compellingly chic," Greene wrote. "The playpen of the quality media set became an Obligatory Scene. The Beautiful People clotted there, light bounding off perfect capped smiles, making midnight Second Avenue bright as noon. Limos . . . vomiting stars, superstars— Mastroianni, Clint Eastwood, John Lennon—and the ultimate wow of the Sixties—Jackie. Inevitably in their wake came the third-string royalty and the second-string rich—the politician and flacks, the sycophants, the voyeurs, the grubs, and slugs and drones, the curious . . . Blueblood dandies and Dun and Bradstreet-adored dudes screamed for See and Be Seen Tables, but Elaine kept them iced at the bar—a gorgon guarding those sexy front stations for her boys. The night everyone's memories fondle gleefully: Henry

Ford and the dazzling Christina cooling at the bar, then exiled to the Ragu Room, Elaine's Siberia. If you are only a simple insecure scrivener with typewriter ink on fingers, who else pampers you at the expense of a Ford?"

Her boys. Here, thought St. George, was a key to her mood. He knew she was happiest when the old crowd was out in force, the writers and journalists whose checks she'd cashed when no one else would, whose early morning rages against editors, publishers, and each other she'd suffered through in sympathetic silence in the days before they—and she—had become legends, before the limos began to show up with royalty from four continents, before Suzy and the cool upper reaches of Hollywood, fashion, jet-set, and social-register society all began to demand the best tables in the front dining room—only to be rejected, humiliated, and come back for more.

God, what a perfectly Olympian assemblage of brilliant and talented and famous people it was tonight, Stuart St. George thought to himself. There were Jack and David and Bruce and Mary and just about everyone Gael Greene had celebrated as an authentic regular: and Bob and Larry and Bobby and Emile and Eleanor and David and Kurt and Jill all at the big central table reserved for the lit-crowd, Old Faithful. Surrounding them and their satellites were constellations of tables glittering with the presence of Princess Diane and Bobby and Swifty and Chessy and

Mica and Ahmet and Princess Dahlia, the fashionable Hollywood elite, drawn to Elaine's by the Algonquin-like aura of class Elaine had created, earning their tables by feeding the egos and bank accounts of the lit crowd with flattery and six-figure screenrights deals. Swirling throughout were a select crew of shady characters, sycophants, and jet-set flotsam—part-time pimps, publicists, even an occasional dealer. And tonight George Plimpton had piloted a dazzling collection of dinner guests directly over here before the demitasse had cooled. So when Princess Lee arrived with her dinner party guests with their mixture of Hapsburg, White House, and Pulitzer titles—well, thought St. George, could Gatsby's parties have been better?

St. George fancied himself something of a young Fitzgerald figure, loved to play the romantic dandy, wore a dinner jacket all the time so that people would assume he was always on his way to or coming from an elegant dinner party.

And, he thought, draining the Pernod, here I am again in the midst of the best and brightest nonstop dinner party there ever was, the place where the moveable feast moved in for good.

Oh, the incandescence of it all! It was right here that the most sophisticated tastes, fashions, and opinions were being forged—and not just for New York, but for America, for Western Civilization itself. Of course, he might be going a little overboard. After all,

Jackie didn't come tonight. And he knew Solzhenitsyn was in town but hadn't put in an appearance. Of course, the cynics would make tasteless jokes about Elaine sticking the Russian exile in the unfashionable dining-room annex popularly known as "Siberia."

People were so unfair, St. George was fond of saying, when they accused Elaine of snobbism and arrogance and rudeness in refusing tables to mere mortals, occasionally even uprooting lesser celebs in the midst of meals to make room for famous favorites. People didn't understand the delicate, subtle alchemy of celebrity, St. George would say. They didn't know that the fierce vigilance with which Elaine watched over the entrance to her dining room, the obsessive care with which she orchestrated the hierarchy of seating arrangements within—that all of this was *essential* to protect this fragile communion of talent and celebrity from being overrun by gawkers and groupies. "Creatures of great salons are great *artists*," St. George had once exclaimed to Danny the bartender late one night when, he hoped, Elaine might overhear.

"What a total crock," Danny had remarked at the close of this encomium. "Hey, that House of Fame. Is that the one in L.A. down Wilshire from the House of Pies?" Not because he disagreed, but because he didn't like gossip columnists who sat on the bar stool and tried to suck up to Elaine. "Stool pigeons," he called them. Since he retired from what he called the "import-export business," Danny had been with Elaine off and on for many years, mainly off, in the Caribbean and South America. He did a lot of fill-in work bartending for Elaine in the summer.

Danny was one of that breed of Golden Boy bartenders who served more than drinks. There's a circuit of select bars, select drugs, and select women. It runs from the Virgin Islands and Key West, up to Aspen, across to some places like Elaine's where the clients combine more advanced tastes and higher bank accounts, much to the profit of the bartenders of the circuit. Having just returned from Belize with the very comfortable profits of an important intermediary function in the export and import of some white powder, Danny had retired from the business and worked the bar for the pure pleasure of the social-sexual chemistry of the celebrity array.

Seeing that it was past three, Danny began to collect the bar tabs from the stool pigeons and close up the register. It had been, he had to admit, a grand old-fashioned night.

He couldn't figure out why so many of the real heavies had shown up on this night. He'd never seen it so crowded on Sunday in August. He knew a lot of these people had left their cool ocean-front homes in the Hamptons to be here tonight and he couldn't figure out why. The chemistry was strange, very loud, very excited, but somehow this was different in character from the churning momentum of the old-fashioned ego orgy he was accustomed to. There was an edge of hysterical gaiety he couldn't figure out. And of course the astonishing reappearance of Walter Foster had thrown everyone off. When Walter Foster walked in, it was one of those awkward moments when nobody knew how to behave—nobody wanted to make a scene but nobody knew a good way of avoiding it.

Danny had been behind the bar that legendary night two years ago, the night Walter Foster had stalked out white-faced after snarling an expletive at Elaine. That humiliating moment marked the bottom line in Foster's precipitous fall from the pinnacle of New York media celebrity—and until this night he had not returned to the scene of that defeat.

Once not long ago when Walter Foster walked into Elaine's, the incandescence within brightened another magnitude, the very air around him crackled with visions of hot books, big deals, the secret intrigues of the famous and powerful. Talented young women glowed when he told them he'd make them stars. And he did. He made a lot of people stars. Writers and directors and TV people. The new media royalty. Trendmakers, tastemakers, image-makers. Certifiable members of Agnew's elite corps of effete intellectual snobs. They all rose with Walter Foster's fortunes. His media empire—trend-setting magazines, hot paperback and publishing properties, independent production companies—was a magic wand in his hands, spotlighting anyone, transforming them into stars. Making or breaking graven images by calculation or whim.

Danny had heard the story of the rise of Walter Foster told and retold at the bar in the furious weeks following the famous Table Incident. How he burst out of the bull market of the mid-Sixties, making first a small fortune in glamour stocks, then a large one selling short the issues he originally rode to glory, as the bear market of the Seventies brought them back to book value.

How he was among the first to figure out that the smart investment for the emerging shape of the Seventies was not glamour stocks but Glamour itself. A profitable commodity. How he played Elaine's like a commodity market. Getting to know the brokers of talent, the smart guys, the insiders, first. Then making his moves. He began to invest in writers, personalities, celebrities, the way he had in the market, picking underpriced talent with potential, promoting it, building the image.

Transforming his image-making power to real power. Fear of his front-cover wrath made the rich and powerful seek out Foster's friendship and favor. Foster would let out the word that one of his angry young stars was preparing a profile of a certain powerful figure, and, soon enough, said figure was likely to make a humble pilgrimage to Elaine's and seek a place at Foster's special table to demonstrate with much conviviality how much he would like to be Foster's friend, to feed Foster's ego while Foster fed himself fettucini.

That table in the rear of the front room was the

symbol of Walter Foster's power and his downfall. In the heady days when he was the highest-rolling winner in the publishing industry, spinning off new magazines, books, publishing companies, transforming himself into a voracious "leisure conglomerate," Elaine made sure that Walter Foster's table was always cleared, set and *empty*, unless Walter Foster was there to sit at it. No matter how many celebrities waited in line hungrily, that table remained empty even if Foster never showed up. It was the ultimate badge of status in Elaine's elaborate hierarchy of favors and attentions—Foster was even more powerful when he *didn't* show up. Of course, throughout the mid-Seventies he almost always showed up to hold court.

He caught the crest of the wave of media fever that engulfed mid-Seventies America. Woodward and Bernstein brought down a President; Redford and Hoffman enshrined the heroic reporters as symbolic successors. The entire journalism profession swelled with newly inflated prestige, power, and self-esteem. Reporters ruled the roost in Washington and New York. They took on the CIA, the FBI—they even took on Hollywood. TV journalists became hot properties of movie-star magnitude. Behind-the-scenes media moguls like Fred Silverman and Katherine Graham became household words.

Meanwhile, the media industry was growing more like the movie capital. Writers acted like stars, editors like directors, publishers like producers. And they all

acted like a new aristocracy. Questions of status became increasingly important. All knights of the
roundtable were theoretically equal, but by the late
Seventies, a place at Walter Foster's table was like a
seat at the right hand of King Arthur himself.

It was at this point that Walter Foster decided to
shake the whole kingdom at its roots. He created a
magazine called *Media Confidential* and proceeded to
throw that entire elite of Elaine's into turmoil.

Of course, as he would later say, the Media Confidential Serial Scandal was all a very logical development. If media people were becoming movie-starlike
public celebrities, then there existed an untapped
public appetite for intimate knowledge of their private
lives, secret loves and hates, and rivalries and scandals.

Shrewdly, Walter Foster felt the time had come to
investigate the investigators, get behind the image of
the image-makers, review the reviewers, get the gossip
on the gossip columnists, and publicize the private
lives of their publishers.

The first few issues of the magazine seemed innocent enough—more a *People* magazine of the media
than anything else, to help establish the cast of characters. But before long the profiles began to get beneath
the skin.

He was just doing to the potentates of the press
what they did daily to everyone else. He hired private
investigators to "review" the private lives of film
critics. He sought out and exposed the hypocrisies and

peccadilloes of the most moralistic investigative reporters, he sought to keep in the public spotlight the
private lives of rival media titans, arguing that he was
only doing to the press what the press did to everyone
else. He made the competitive envy and family feuds
within media institutions the subject of as much fer-
vent attention as sports and politics elsewhere. He'd
hire teams of media critics to savage the prose, the
grammar, the accuracy of the leading lights of the profession. He began to publish thinly fictionalized
romans à clef about celebrity journalists, media moguls, and the status, then he'd publish articles analyz-
ing the novels and pointing out who the real people
were in case there were any mistakes. It began to look as
if in all those years of gathering gossip at Elaine's he
had accumulated something on everyone. At first, of
course, he kept the Elaine's regulars off-limits to his
muckraking of the muckrakers. In fact, he persuaded
some of his best writers from the Elaine's crowd to go
after his targets. It's all in good clean fun, he said.

It was when he began publishing a serialized
novel about Elaine's itself in the pages of *Media
Confidential* that some people stopped having fun.
A low-down Capote-like betrayal of privacy, they
screamed. Foster was using the most intimate and
delicious secrets confided in the camaraderie of long,
late nights at Elaine's. The thinly disguised serial
revealed confidences with irrevocable consequences—
who stole whose ideas, and whose wife; what writer X

really said to his close friends about writer Y's talent and how writer Z engineered a hatchet job on writer X's book last time out; who really betrayed who in the entangled history of Famous Feuds. Husbands and wives would read about affairs their partners had conducted five years ago for the first time in the pages of Walter Foster's magazine. Friendships foundered as friends suspected each other of sharing their secrets for display in the infamous Media Confidential Serial. The whole thing might have become unmanageably explosive had not the serial been terminated when Walter Foster suddenly gambled away and lost his entire media empire.

"Eyes bigger than stomach," was the epitaph the Wall Street guys gave to the Big Apple Bubble, as it came to be called. Foster had his eyes on taking over a dying but heavily capitalized movie studio. Maybe he wanted to be The Last Tycoon in addition to Citizen Kane. He tried a power play with a tender offer, found himself in over his head in a bidding war and had to raise cash by selling control of his original magazine to another conglomerate. He lost the fight for control of the movie company; he lost the backing of his own money people. The new controlling interest bought up his contract and sent him packing from his magazine.

For a while he continued to come to Elaine's. At first it was exciting, like Napoleon at Elba, in a way. Dynamic new plans were floated—for financing a comeback, for revenge. Loyal lieutenants brought reports from the captive territories soon to be reconquered. It was going to be grand. But there were difficulties. The money people didn't share the grandiosity of his vision. The longer things stalled, the more irritable he grew at his powerlessness. He no longer had the power to commission and kill profiles, so courtesy calls at his table paid him by politicians, he realized, were actually paid out of courtesy now, not fear. People did not walk across the room past potentates and powers to stop at Walter Foster's table *first*. He began to absent himself more frequently, sometimes a week at a time.

Then late one night, after a particularly long absence, he walked into Elaine's and halfway across the crowded dining room before he stopped dead in his tracks. *Somebody was sitting at his table.* And most galling of all to Walter Foster was that it was not just somebody, it was that upstart Jann Wenner, smiling and lifting his glass to Foster, toasting him from his own table. Foster turned, stalked out snarling, never to return. Until tonight.

The humiliating incident had been the talk of the town for months back then. The general verdict was that Elaine was perfectly justified. "How could she keep the table empty forever, it's not the Tomb of the Unknown Soldier, for Chrissakes," someone remarked. And somehow after that wound Walter Foster was never the same. The life bled out of his comeback. He never got it off the ground.

But why, then, Danny the bartender wondered, would Walter Foster show up tonight out of the blue? Why risk Elaine's wrath and further humiliation? What's going on?

Fortunately, Danny could see Elaine was not going to waste time further humiliating Foster. She was in a benevolent mood. After sufficient hesitation, to make sure he realized that what followed was a charitable benefice, Elaine embraced Foster formally and held out her hand to the striking woman in the white linen suit who accompanied him.

Heads turned and voices hushed in that crowded dining room as Elaine led the couple straight to Foster's old table, which, whether by accident or design, was just being cleared. Foster seated himself on the chair facing the wall. Another little surprise to the cognoscenti. In the old days he invariably sat with his back to the wall, the better to receive courtiers—although some wise guy said that, like Wild Bill Hickock, Foster had too many enemies to turn his back to a crowded room.

But tonight he did. Maybe he didn't want to face that excited, inquisitive, feral crowd. Those regulars who did catch a glimpse of Foster on his passage across the room were shocked at how dramatically his features had changed since his last, ill-fated visit. Indeed everything that had been ruddy, vital, even apoplectic about Foster seemed to have been drained from him. His features now were pale, puffy and slack.

"It's the ghost of Christmas past," slurred the alcoholic playwright seated with Princess Rizzoli at the table behind Foster's.

There had been talk about Foster's behavior since the fall. He was said to be embittered and obsessed with vengeance upon those who had, he claimed, tricked and betrayed him out of the empire he built from nothing. And it was peculiar how tonight he said hello to no one, took his seat, and looked only at the woman across from him.

Still, he *had* kept up outer appearances: despite the swelter outside, his blue-and-white-striped seersucker suit was fresh and crisp as the day it was minted in the workrooms of J. Press. Foster had always made a point of dressing as if he had not been rejected by Princeton three decades ago: a kind of perpetual, prep-school, nonchalant elegance. No accessories. Unless you counted the beautiful women with him as accessories. He did.

But that woman with him, a striking woman with jet black hair and green eyes—what was her story? Even Elaine had wondered about her as she seated them. She was beautiful, tanned and tropical in her white linen suit, but she looked half his 50 years and out of place in his world. And very nervous about something.

"You know her?" Stuart St. George asked Danny the bartender, who was staring intently at the lady in the linen suit.

"Yeah, Lauren Bacall. Used to be in pictures."

"Come on. Although I must say there really is something of that quality about her. And those green eyes. You do know her, don't you?"

"No. Wish I did though."

He did.

Once, three years ago in the Florida Keys. A Prohibition-era mansion on a privately owned key. Built originally, so the locals said, by old Joe Kennedy for dealings with certain figures in the smuggling trade before Repeal. Sheltered deep-water docking facilities and all that. Danny was there on a business trip—this was before an unfortunate circumstance forced him out of the import-export trade.

She owned the place. Either she or her lover, a former Nicaraguan diplomat turned cocaine smuggler who claimed descent from a black-sheep branch of the Somoza family. If, in fact, he was her lover and not merely a business partner. The seaplane pilot who stepped onto the deck with two attaché cases packed with large bills may well have been both.

The long hot afternoon on which the deal had gone down had been confusing, albeit highly profitable in many ways. He couldn't even remember what she'd been calling herself—was it Lilah? But there was something she did that afternoon he'd never forget—

even now, as it dawned on him that the woman in the white linen dress was the woman he'd met on the key, he felt a throb of lust as he recalled the scene.

Negotiations had been droning on as they sometimes will in the parlor room; bills were counted, kilograms were weighed. She had absented herself to deepen her tan on the sundeck. Two hours later she reappeared, cocoa butter and sweat glistening on those parts of her body not covered by a delicately crafted, mesh bikini. From inside an oiled walnut breakfront she removed a leather case once intended for heirloom silverware, took it to a chaise next to the negotiating table, and opened it to reveal two powerful handguns wrapped in soft gun cloth resting atop the blue velvet lining.

One was a .357 magnum pistol, the other a Luger. Humming to herself, working slowly and expertly, she took each gun apart, cleaned it, oiled the parts, adjusted the firing mechanisms, spun the barrels, loaded them with cartridges, put them together, and wrapped them back up.

It was, he recalled, a hypnotic and erotic performance. No wonder he couldn't forget her. But what could she be doing now? he wondered as he turned to the cash register to begin totaling up for the night. Any why with Walter Foster? He was still working on that question when the lights went out and all hell broke loose.

Later the homicide cops would establish the fact

that at 3:22 A.M. someone ripped the fuses out of the
fuse box in Elaine's basement, plunging the assembled
celeb illuminati into a sudden dark democracy wherein
no proper distinction or recognition of degree could
be observed.

"Danny, for God's sake, get me a flashlight,"
Elaine called out to her bartender.

"Can't see to find the fucker," said Danny.

"Time to pay Con Ed," someone ventured. A
nervous laugh rippled across the dark room.

People began to relax. For a moment it looked as
if this would turn into one of those jolly catastrophes
the newspapers love, with everyone showing true New
York ésprit and wit and all that. A nice feature for the
Times' style page. Liz Smith, Suzy, and Page Six would
have fun with it.

Then, in the center of the room, the sound of a
crash, shattering glass and shrieks of pain as a table for
four, heavily laden with dishes, was violently upended.
Somewhere in the room a woman screamed hysteri-
cally, *"No. Please.* He's got a *gun."*

"Everybody out. Now," a man's voice yelled. Up
front someone threw a chair through the window,
climbed out and started screaming for help. In the
noise and confusion and panic of the exodus no one
heard the shot. That's what silencers are for.

Ten minutes later the tastemakers of Western
Civilization were regrouping themselves outside the
darkened restaurant amid the broken glass, the steamy

mist, and the Silver Clouds. Danny the bartender was looking in vain for the girl in the white linen suit. Only Anthony the chauffeur, from his special vantage point in the phone booth, saw her disappear around the corner. Someone had finally located a flashlight and Elaine was preparing to reenter when Princess Dahlia discovered the blood on her shawl.

It was a cream-colored, raw-silk shawl. A favorite. When the lights went out and the panic began she grabbed it off the back of her chair, trailing it behind her in the rush to the exit. It was only when she stumbled out of the darkened restaurant and slipped the shawl over her bare shoulders that she felt something warm and wet soaking through the raw silk.

It was not royal blood: the Brazilian surgeon quickly determined that it had not come from any wound on the body of the Princess.

In the midst of the shrill frenzy out on the sidewalk, George Plimpton himself plucked the blood-stained shawl from the gutter where the Princess had dropped it. He seemed undecided as to whether it would be more gentlemanly to return it to the Princess or dispose of it himself, when Elaine snatched it out of his hands and started back into her shattered restaurant with the flashlight gleaming in one hand, the bloody silk in the other. Sweeping aside hands that tried to restrain her, ignoring pleas that she wait for the police, Elaine stalked right in.

It didn't take her long to find him. He was still

there at his special table—well, under it. When the flashlight beam first fell upon his form stretched out, face-up amid the debris of broken chairs, plates, and bottles, she thought he might be playing some bizarre joke on her. "What the hell are you doing lying here, Foster?" she was about to say. Then, as she picked her way toward him, she looked more closely, running the flashlight slowly up the length of the still figure. His black Guccis still gleamed like polished onyx, his seersucker slacks still held a knife-edge crease. His tie was neatly anchored in place by a gleaming ruby stickpin, and the knot was centered perfectly in his collar.

But wait. That ruby gleam. It occurred to Elaine that Walter Foster had never been the type to wear jeweled stickpins. At last she reached Walter Foster's special table and saw the blood slowly leaking into a pool beneath his body from—as the coroner would later report—a ragged exit hole torn out of his back by a .38 caliber bullet. That ruby gleam had been the neat entry wound. No ruby stickpin. Walter Foster would have died before permitting himself to appear so unfashionable.

THE NARRATIVE
OF GUY DAVENPORT

Now, I'm not trying to hide the fact that I was smoking the Big O that night. If you want to know the truth, by the time Lilah French burst into my apartment that early A.M. hour I was three hefty pipefuls deep into some highly potent Golden Triangle black opium. And that is very deep.

That treacherous poppy gum. If I hadn't been so deep in a trance at the time, I'm sure I wouldn't have been so easily seduced into becoming an accomplice in her escape attempt. And if I'd kept my nose clean then I wouldn't have been so easily silenced by the coverup that followed, forced to forego the biggest scoop that ever came my way, compelled to write this account not for publication but for deposit in a bank vault where it will remain unread unless certain parties attempt to make good on certain ill-advised threats.

But before I begin with Lilah French and the death of Walter Foster, I want to make one thing clear about this opium smoking of mine. Because credibility is important to me. This account won't have much insurance value for me if it can be dismissed as an opium-fogged fantasy.

So it's important to me that no one get the wrong impression about my use of opium on that particular evening. It was not in any sense a *recreational* indulgence. I was not wallowing in poppy stupor for the purpose of self-gratification. I was engaged in research of a serious and scholarly nature, a piece of literary detection that had led me to a sensational discovery—a murder scandal of far greater consequence to literary history than the murder of Walter Foster, although try to convince these trendy magazine editors around town. All they'll want to hear about is the murder at Elaine's.

Now I realize there are those who might snicker when I call my opium smoking "research." For instance, those familiar with the byline "Guy Davenport" from the pages of the youth culture's *Argonaut* magazine where my drug-crazed accounts of adventures covering presidential campaigns have been chronicled. I know if anyone recognizes the name they're likely to recall a notorious but much-misunderstood episode in my journalistic career. "Guy Davenport," you'll say, "Isn't that the guy who dropped acid on the President's plane?"

Well, that just shows you how distorted some of these accounts are you hear in the press. First of all, I hardly ever take LSD anymore. As a matter of fact, contrary to the impression one might get from the pages of *Argonaut* (an impression I won't deny I try to create), I don't even like drugs very much. I'm just under a lot of pressure from these goddamn editors to act crazy. You know the syndrome with these New York magazine editors. They sit in their offices and they read some great pieces of writing like the ones Hunter Thompson turned out during the '72 campaign and the only thing they can think is: "I want one of those for *my* magazine." Now to tell the truth, I've sampled a few controlled substances in my time, but I don't really enjoy taking drugs that much anymore. But if that's what the editors want, it's a living. Some people get up in the morning and go to work and sell mutual funds; some people get up and stuff themselves with drugs and freak out at public events. Now as for that acid I dropped, everyone knows that it's almost impossible to get the genuine article today. And next, as I clearly explained in my account of the story, I didn't "drop" that one little tablet I had—didn't swallow it, that is. I had been sitting in my seat in the Press Section of Air Force One trying to figure out how to relieve the tedium on the flight from Orlando, Florida, to Champaign-Urbana, Illinois (the Prez was campaigning in both the Florida and Illinois primaries that fateful weekend in February '76) and I had taken the little tablet out of its tinfoil just to make sure it was still there, and as I was raising it to eye level to gaze at the little barrel-shaped beauty, I dropped it, literally dropped it, on the carpet in the aisle of the fuselage.

So naturally I started crawling around on my hands and knees, looking for it, perfectly prepared to chew up the entire carpet to get it into my system, when who should decide to appear for an informal press conference but President Gerald Ford himself, flanked by a grim group of Secret Service guys, looking at me like I needed to explain myself.

"Just looking for a contact lens," I said looking up from the carpet. I realized too late this may have sounded a bit lame, since I was wearing mirrored sunglasses at the time.

"Didn't know you wore contacts, four-eyes," one of them said pleasantly. He had a point there—I don't.

"Well, actually I don't wear contacts," I said. "But I thought if I found one down here I'd try it on and see if I liked it."

Christ, there I go wandering into the past again like a punch-drunk fighter gibbering in his gin. (Christ, there I go using expletives like "Christ!" and macho metaphors like "punch-drunk fighter"—you have to excuse me, but once you start imitating the great Dr. Thompson, it's hard to stop.)

But there's a point to setting the record straight here. I don't want people to be misled by the alleged acid-drop into mistrusting my judgment and perspective, the *credibility* of my account of the extraordinary events I am about to relate. I really don't like to take drugs. I am a bookish and scholarly sort at heart. I prefer to spend my time in Dickens' London rather than Abe Beame's New York. And so, when I tell you that I was smoking that potent Golden Triangle and rubbed black opium only as a necessary adjunct to a sophisticated and scholarly piece of literary detection, I want people to understand that this is no Guy Davenport joke. This is serious business. Perhaps I should explain just how serious.

You see, I had solved the fictional Mystery of Edwin Drood and, in the process, discovered not merely the solution to a literary riddle but the key to a ghastly real-life murder that has been covered up for more than a century.

Maybe some of you weren't aware that the Mystery of Edwin Drood hadn't been solved. But, you see, Charles Dickens never finished his last novel. He dropped dead in the middle of serializing it. Precisely in the middle. Dickens had just completed the sixth of a projected twelve monthly installments of *The Mystery of Edwin Drood* when, on June 9, 1870, he suddenly collapsed and died—an "apoplectic stroke brought on by exhaustion," it was said at the time. There was no autopsy.

I'd been studying the Drood problem on and off for some years. Before they kicked me out of school (a totally trumped-up charge of acid-dealing; I wasn't dealing, I was giving it away. The only thing I was dealing was a little grass), I had begun researching a senior thesis on solutions to "the Drood problem," as Dickensians call it: exactly how Dickens would have brought the novel to a close had he lived.

After studying the solutions proposed by a century of Drood investigators—the great Holmes himself tried his hand at it—I was convinced that all of them lacked inevitability. None of them made you slam down the book and declare, "This is *it*, this is what Dickens was up to and this is how he'd do it."

Of course, everyone who has studied the case agrees that the man who murdered young Edwin Drood was John Jasper, the oily, opium-smoking choirmaster who had designs on Drood's fiancée, Miss Rosa Bud. (Some have speculated that, in "Citizen Kane," Orson Welles chose Rosebud as the objective correlative of the unsolved mystery of Charles Foster Kane as an allusion to the similarly arcane mystery of Drood.) Although everyone agrees that John Jasper is the villain, several serious areas of controversy remain over the outcome of the novel. Is young Drood actually dead, or has he fled the dread designs of John Jasper to seek safety? Has Jasper revealed what he did to Drood, to Princess Puffer, the senile proprietress of the opium den he frequents? How will Helena Landless, the beautiful half-breed from Ceylon (and one of the few overtly sensual women in Dickens' work) save her twin brother from being framed by Jasper for the murder? And Datchery, the mysterious stranger who appears near the end of the last installment completed before Dickens' death—could he be the resourceful Helena in male disguise?

Finally, I became convinced that the only way to get to the heart of the darkness with Drood and Dickens himself was to perform a series of literary experiments with opium. The nature of these experiments was suggested by the solution of a mystery novel by Dickens' protégé Wilkie Collins. In *The Moonstone,* which Collins published shortly before *Drood* (and which T.S. Eliot calls the "first and greatest English detective novel") Collins' hero takes opium in an attempt to re-create his state of mind on the night of the crime.

Now, it is well known that at the time they published those mystery novels, both Collins and Dickens were heavy users of laudanum, a widely available tincture of opium preparation. And so, it is not unreasonable to conjecture that Dickens planned to use the opium subplot to smoke out the secret of Drood's disappearance from John Jasper.

As you might have guessed, I decided it was absolutely necessary for me to begin smoking opium while reading Drood in order to re-create the state of mind of the opium-smoking choirmaster at that time. Unfortunately, I began this series of experiments under conditions that were less than ideal. My editors at *Argonaut* were pressing me to return to the campaign trail and write wild and crazy things about my adventures thereon. So I packed opium pipe, my annotated copy of *Drood,* and the Golden Triangle black that had come to me via diplomatic pouch from Singapore, courtesy of an old Vietnam hand now in the State Department who traded me even up for some organic mescaline I happened to have lying around.

Night after night, in one motel room after another, while the other reporters filed overnight reports on the nonevents or played practical jokes on Ron Nessen, I would tell the switchboard to refuse all calls, particularly those from my editors in New York, and return to my room to puff my pipe and pursue the phantomlike psyche of John Jasper.

The more opium I smoked, the deeper the trance in which I meditated upon passages from Drood, the more I began to sense a set of implications, entirely unexpected and very, very strange, stir and emerge from the substrata beneath the text. At first there were hints, then horrifying flashes of intuition, then a growing coherent suspicion. And then, one night in the Peoria Hilton I found the clue. Yes, the Peoria Hilton. I'd been traveling with "The Bozo Special," as the reporters on board had called the Ford campaign plane. The Illinois primary was drawing to a soporific close, and while the President was out addressing a banquet of sorghum growers, I was high above the skyline of Peoria (I had an eighth-floor room) transfixed by an incredible opium-trance revelation. To wit: Dickens had discovered, in the course of writing the monthly installments of *Drood*, that someone was out to murder *him*. Yes, to murder Charles Dickens himself because of some thinly disguised dark revelations Dickens had made in the early installments of *Drood:* to prevent Dickens from completing the novel and revealing anything more. That for some reasons of blackmail or fear of scandal Dickens was unable to take the matter to the authorities. Instead, his only recourse was to slip into the text of *Drood* certain hints and clues to identify the nemesis threatening his life.

That night in the Peoria Hilton, deep in my poppy trance, I was astonished to see Dickens himself appear in the cathedral town in which *Drood* is set, lead me to the top of the bell tower, and begin to reveal to me himself the name of the man who engineered his murder. At that point, the bells began a deafening clang, drowning the words of my apparition, shattering the vision. It was, it turned out, my hotel room phone and, at the other end, the angry shouting of the editor of *Argonaut*. He pointed out to me that I had run up some $20,000 in expenses covering the presidential campaign so far and had yet to indicate whether I intended to write anything.

"Goddamn you!" I yelled into the phone. "I'm on the trail of the fucker who murdered Charles Dickens—it's the literary crime of the century—and I'm about to nail the bastard who did it, and you call and ask me about *expenses*. You'll go down in history lower than the jerk-off who interrupted Coleridge. Fuck the campaign—I've got serious work to do!"

That ended my long association with *Argonaut*. Since then, court papers from three magazines demanding return of expenses in five figures have arrived at my door. The last woman who could stand being around this mania left me last week, making some crack about Lee Harvey Oswald doing Dickens in.

My only sexual experiences since then have been some increasingly intense and erotic opium-dream meetings with the lithe, tigerish—and fictional— Helena Landless in settings from *Drood*.

Now, I know it's beginning to sound as if I were in the grip of a deranged obsession, but the textual and biographical evidence will vindicate me when I publish my monograph on the subject. I'm convinced I may have to publish my findings myself, and when I do there will be more than a dozen editors at publishing houses and magazine offices around New York who will finally realize how shortsighted and narrow-minded they were to turn down my offer of exclusive rights to these dramatic revelations about the death of Charles Dickens.

Anyway, obsession or not, I was determined to continue pursuing my opium research until I recaptured the answer Dickens almost gave me that night in Peoria.

And so, sometime around midnight that Sunday night, the night Walter Foster would be shot to death at Elaine's, I began to make my usual research preparations. By that time I had a little ritual I liked to follow. I'd draw the curtains of my snug, but shabby, little fifth-floor studio overlooking Gramercy Park. I'd light a devotional candle left over from the blackout. I unplugged my phone to frustrate deadline-obsessed editors and debt-demanding creditors who liked nothing better than to harass me late at night.

Already anticipating the cozy warmth of the opium glow rolling up my spine, I changed into the faded-silk dressing gown I preferred for opium sessions. I'd gotten it years ago, an unwanted going-away present from a well-to-do roommate on the day I was expelled. Made by Brooks Brothers in one of their rare mad moments, it had the look of Sydney Greenstreet seediness now. I sank down in the huge old horsehair settee that had probably been a fixture of this ancient brownstone since the 1840's when Edgar Allen Poe lived some months on the ground floor.

I picked up my pipe. I picked up my annotated

copy of *Drood,* the Penguin edition. I set the black
gum aglow and drew in the sweet vapors as I opened
the book and began reading a particularly provocative
and puzzling passage about Helena Landless. According to Edmund Wilson, Dickens had modeled this
wild and delicate creature upon his most passionate
extramarital attachment. Her lithe and powerful sensuality comes through with a direct erotic force unlike
anything in Dickens' previous fiction. Believe me, I
know. You see, on opium one does not have what the
Boy Scout handbook calls a "wet dream." One can,
however, have an extraordinarily sensual and fleshy
experience. Something like a tryst with the legendary
succubus. It happened that night with Helena Landless. After three pipefuls. It was as real as sex could be
with a fictional character. We were in the bell tower of
the cathedral, high above the crypt where Jasper
murders Drood.

You find yourself doing strange things in an
opium dream. I was accustomed to drifting through
the landscape of *Drood* in my past researches, but
tonight I found myself swinging from the bell rope
in slow motion, sort of Tarzan-style, legs entwined
around the rope, the long, burnished golden legs of
Helena Landless entwined about me. Up and back we
swung. Chimes rang out, rang out in response to our
rhythmic swings. There is a legend among gourmet
drug aficionados that one has not felt the One True
and Perfect Clarity of the Cocaine Rush until one has

heard the choir of musical chimes that peal out of the vibratory ecstasy of each neuron in the central nervous system. Then, there's the earthy ghetto expression of the ultimate in sexual satiety—"that little lady can really ring my chimes." I was blissfully immersed in the ringing of my chimes when the chimes became discordant, insistent, dysrhythmic, and I realized that someone was jamming frantically at my doorbell.

Startled out of my trance, I looked at my clock. Chimes at 4 A.M.; I didn't like it. My paranoid computer shuddered into action and chattered out the awful possibilities: The Secret Service had caught up with me for some indiscretions I had committed in the course of keeping some of the younger Carter campaign aides supplied with herb. A collection agent from one of the dope dealers I still owe money to for fronting me the kilos for Carter's campaign staff.

As I stumbled to the foyer, I still wasn't sure what was going on inside my head and what was outside my door. Keeping the safety chain fastened, I creaked the door open two inches and put my eye to the crack.

Something large and powerful blasted the door open from the outside, tearing the chain off its hinges, smacking me viciously in the forehead and knocking me to the floor. Something massive and snarling leaped on me. I felt my neck seized and held by seething incisors that threatened multiple puncture wounds each time I so much as inhaled or exhaled— and I wasn't doing much of that.

Then I heard a lilting West Texas drawl over the growls. "My goodness, Khan, I'm afraid you've given the nice man a scare. Git. Sit over there. The nice man is our friend, and we want him to help us."

"Hello, Lilah," I said, when the beast—a Scottish deerhound, I think they call the huge, savage animals—freed my jugular. "The nice man would like to put the big dog to sleep.... Hey, why are you here?"

She knelt down and touched the swelling on my· forehead and stroked my jaw. "Precious one, I am *so* sorry for this. Khan is a very sensitive and chivalrous dog. He senses that tonight I am very much a damsel in distress, and he wants desperately to prove his devotion to me."

"So I noticed."

"He's so sweet and well-intentioned. But so are you, darling. And I have come to take advantage of you. I need help, and I am doing something that may be dangerous. I need to get myself and certain items safely out of town before at least two groups of people—one of them being the police—find either me or those items. Now, I can't hope from you the gallantry of Khan, but if memories of bright college years are not enough to motivate you, I am prepared to offer you explicit sexual favors in return for your cooperation.

"But before you start asking me questions, make us both some strong black coffee and change into some real clothes. Is there any law that says you have to wear that silly-looking bathrobe when you smoke opium?"

I had to laugh. That was Lilah, all right. She had that knack of throwing up at you the bewildering repertoire of the Texas woman: mock raillery, mock coquettishness and several varieties of seductiveness, which kept you guessing which was the real and which the mock. Except that underneath it all was a flinty, high-prairie stoicism that was very real and very tough.

Not that she grew up in some sod house. Her father was one of the biggest wildcatters out of Dalhart, Texas. Owned half the Panhandle before he moved to Palm Beach and decided to buy his way into polite society. Failing that, he married Lilah's mother, the closest thing to a wildcat Palm Beach society offered—a member of that select club of women said to have slept with Joseph Kennedy, both Senior and Junior.

In fact, there had been some talk that Lilah was really the child of one or the other. All of which gave her a special cachet when she transferred to Yale from whatever Swiss *école* her mother had stashed her away at. Swiftly she became a legend in New York, as well as in New Haven. Her Park Avenue triplex became the scene of masked balls and decadent private parties. She dazzled the Romance Language department with her mastery of early Provençal poetics and delighted the visionary company on campus when she returned one spring from Basel with a gram of pure Sandoz LSD she claimed she had stored in a safe-deposit vault when the pharmaceuticals firm stopped production.

That was how we met. I was otherwise out of her league, but in certain circles I had a reputation for a gourmet sensibility when it came to such compounds, and one day that spring she invited me to share a trip.

I promptly fell deeply in love with the entire expanding universe, and particularly the breathtaking shimmer of it in her wide, green eyes. She fell in love with the universe in general, but not with me, in particular. She said she felt our souls had merged so completely on the trip there was no need for our bodies to go through the formalities. It sounded good at the time. It was only after I came down I realized that was the way certain women say, "I've got a headache tonight." We did form one of those bonds of acid kinship from that trip together but, she explained, I couldn't offer her the adventure and the danger she seemed to be looking for.

In the middle of her senior year she ran off with someone who could. He called himself a diplomat, had been Nicaraguan consul in New York—he was a Somoza—but was up to his neck in mutinous intrigue against the ruling branch of his family. There were stories of trade in guns and other substances that enter the country in fast hydrofoil boats. Then there were stories about his arrest and her escape.

I'd lost track of her until the Republican National

Convention of 1972, the coronation of Richard Nixon in Miami, when I ran into her in the elevator of the Fontainebleau Hotel. She got off at a floor heavily guarded by Secret Servicemen in the company of a married man who was later rumored to be Woodward and Bernstein's "Deep Throat." The next day, afraid I might publish his name in my usual irresponsible journalistic way, she looked me up. We had dinner a few times, and several long and inconclusive evenings, but I'd never been able to sort out which of the stories about her was true and what she was really after. Had she inherited the Somozas' smuggling connections and staffed them with expert women couriers and dealers? Had she flown to North Africa and spent a year in Morocco trying to shift the sexual attentions of a brilliant expatriate novelist from native boys to her? Had Dylan written that song ("If you see her, say hello, she may be in Tangier") for her?

Coffee steaming. Joint burning. Beast munching rock-hard frozen hamburger as if it were ladyfingers. Lilah pacing the room waiting for the multiple stimulants to clear the opium glaze from my eyes. Me watching her powerful, graceful movements.

"I'm going to need some of your clothes," she suddenly announced, flinging open my closet door. "Let's see. Corduroys. A shirt from Brooks. Penny loafers. My, my, I knew all along that behind all that decadent talk in *Argonaut* you were still a dear old preppy at heart. I'll pin up my hair; you'll find me a hat. They're going to be looking for a woman in a white linen suit—and no one will even know I'm a woman."

She had been taking her clothes off as she spoke. The white linen skirt was at her feet and she was standing with her back to me, wearing only a thin silk blouse. I felt my appetites revive.

"I'd call that pose a sexual favor already," trying to sound nonchalant as I got up and walked across to her.

She turned to face me, holding a couple of pairs of corduroys over her arm. Reaching out, she tugged at the knot on my dressing gown and drew me up close to her.

"Look," she said softly. "I've been trying to play this scene with you with a light touch, but I'm in some very heavy trouble and don't have much time to get out of it. So let's both put some pants on and talk about it."

She handed me a pair of corduroys. Dutifully, I stepped into them.

She looked up at me. "Okay. In 24 hours I'm probably going to be wanted for murder and I'm going to have to leave the country for an indefinite period of time. The first thing I want you to do is take care of Khan. I'll guarantee he'll be friendly—won't you, beast? Just keep him till I get word to you whether I can come back. If I can't, you can have him put to sleep if you want. Just don't leave him to rot in some god-damn kennel or pet hotel—understand that.

"They're horrible places, and I'd rather he were dead than locked up in one of them for—"

"Wait a minute, Lilah. What are you talking about—what murder?"

"Walter Foster was shot dead in Elaine's tonight. I was sitting with him before it happened. The lights went out. No one saw it happen."

"But wait a minute. Why would they want you? You didn't . . . ?"

"Of course not, but I think he was shot with my gun—it's registered to me—and there will be my fingerprints on it."

"I don't understand."

"I'm not sure I do either, but Foster calls me yesterday and says he needs a gun to protect himself. That someone's been calling and threatening him and that first he thought it was a joke but now he's scared because the caller is giving little hints he's been inside Foster's apartment and knows his daily schedule. So he begs me to bring him a gun. He knows I'm knowledge-able and I still have my husband's collection. I ask him does he want to stop by and pick it up and he says no, that would be too dangerous for me, so he tells me to meet him at Elaine's at a certain time on the dot. With the gun in my purse.

"When I meet him there I know something's very

wrong but he won't say a thing during dinner. Then when the lights go out I pick up my purse to run and it feels empty, because the gun is gone. Then I think I hear a shot and Walter is dead, and I just ran and ran and, well, here I am. You look at me as if you don't believe me. Go ahead, look into my eyes."

"No, no. What I don't understand is why you have to leave town right away. Why don't you just call the cops? Talk to them in a lawyer's office. Tell them the whole story. Then they can start looking for the guy who made the phone threats. Then he's the suspect, not you."

"Well, I wish I could do just that. You don't know how much more at ease my mind would be but there are some other people I'm involved with in a very large business deal at the moment. I've been staying with the beast here at Foster's place while making some last-minute arrangements."

"You mean smuggling? Then what is your relationship with Foster, anyway? Or what was it? I shouldn't ask?"

"It's complicated. Part business, part personal, but nothing like you'd think, although maybe worse. Can we save that for later, because time is running out for this poor cracker child in the big city and I've got one more wish, which if you grant shall place me at your service forever. I have to get down to my place and remove something—some things—fast before the cops find out who I am and what kind of investments I make. One of the bartenders at Elaine's tonight, he was in the trade. He could have recognized me and tipped the cops. They could come busting in while we're there, but I've got to take the risk.

"You have your car. I want you to drive me to my place and take certain packages into safekeeping for me."

"Certain packages?"

"Yes, certain packages. They happen to be labeled Doggie Vitamins. You don't want to know what's in them. Who knows? Maybe your reporter's shield is good for something. Protect your source. Protect me. Coming?"

Outside, the mist had finally precipitated into a sweaty drizzle. We crossed the street to where my aging Dodge squatted by the spiked fence enclosing the locked-up greenery of Gramercy Park. Lilah gazed through the soupy murk at the enclosed garden of perfectly hedged and ordered landscape.

"That was five years ago we spent the night out there, wasn't it, darling? Do you still have a key?"

"Funny thing about that," I said as I opened the passenger door of the Dodge for her. "About three months ago, the trustees of Gramercy Park Neighborhood Committee voted to rescind my key privileges. I've been banned forever. Bunch of self-righteous snoops."

"You mean they observed you camping out with your little girlfriends, I'll bet," she said.

"They claimed they weren't spying, but I know they were. But that wasn't the clincher. It was some house guests of mine, members of a kind of club called the Trenton Road Dogs. They had offered to come over and give me a line by line critique of a piece I was writing about them. Very persuasive editors, these guys. Well, they asked if I could give them a tour of Gramercy Park. They liked it so much they had my key copied and invited some friends of theirs over, but I had no idea it would be the Hell's Angels, and no one told me about any cycle race inside the park . . . ."

"I'm sure you would have stepped right in and dragged them out of there by the scruff of their necks if you had known, my brave one," Lilah cooed sweetly. "Or do they have necks? I know they have scruff."

"I'll introduce you to them sometime," I said, twisting the ignition key savagely and getting only agonized metallic whooping coughs from the engine.

"Took away your precious little key to the park, did they?" Lilah said. "It's funny. That's what happened to poor Walter Foster."

"I didn't know he lived on Gramercy Park," I said. "I'm sure I would have seen—"

"No, darling. They took away his reserved table at Elaine's. In his world that's worse than—oh, it's all so silly," she said. "It's just the Snoosters of Dalhart, Texas, all over again."

"The Whoosters?"

"The Snoosters. Back in my little prairie town,

before Daddy moved us to Palm Beach, my school girlfriends and I had an exclusive club called the Snoosters. We never had a clubhouse; all we did was make up lists of people we wouldn't admit to the Snooster Club and gang up on each other to humiliate the people who were in by kicking them out. It's one of those not-so-nice human instincts Rousseau chose to ignore. I know you New Yorkers think you're so sophisticated but, face it darling, you all have your Snooster Clubs and Clubhouses. Elaine is just the Grand Snooster-in-Chief these days."

"Snoosterhood is powerful," I said.

"Yes," said Lilah. "For some people, it's deadly serious."

I have to admit, I was surprised when the disintegrating Dodge actually started. I didn't use the car to drive; it was more a kind of holding action in a complicated bureaucratic guerrilla war I was waging to preserve my press plates.

Now if you've never been a reporter in New York, you might not understand the importance attached to press plates—ordinary license numbers followed by the magic letters NYP, which permitted parking in strategically located midtown zones forbidden even to DPL plates. Most of the time, press plates allowed you to park in the wrong alternate side of the street zone without being ticketed and towed. That's right, the *wrong* alternate side of the street zones. To some New Yorkers, that meant more in personal power and

prestige than a front table at Elaine's. I could tell
you some scandalous stories about the way non-work-
ing media people, the editors, publishers, and inves-
tors, use their pull to get NYP plates for their goddamn
limos so the chauffeur won't be inconvenienced when
he drives their wives to shop at Bonwit's. What burns
me up is that I had to work three years through the
bureaucratic jungle to finally get my press plates,
and three months later they try to take them away
from me. Because my car was repossessed. It wasn't
even really repossessed; it was just taken away from
me by a dealer who announced that I wouldn't be
needing it to travel. I might not even be able to *walk* if
I didn't pay him some trifling sum that had slipped my
mind. This came at the very time the vindictive
accountant-minded sub-editors at *Argonaut* decided I
hadn't fulfilled some petty requirement or other to
complete my contract and had tried to get my press
plates rescinded because I no longer had an official
media connection. Well, I got the car back, so I had
something to hang the plates on, and I'm still appeal-
ing their revocation, but it's just another example of
the privileged lives these media heavies live. Rich
dilettantes will buy a whole newspaper just to get NYP
plates. None of them are capable of putting one
goddamn word on a blank piece of paper that doesn't
sound as pompous as they are, but they get their NYP
plates just like that. They get all the privileges, the

glamourous image of being part of the press without any of the goddamn work.

If I hadn't been fuming to myself over these injustices as I pulled out of my semi-permanent parking space and headed west on Gramercy Park South, I might not have paid attention to the green Rolls limo double-parked north of the intersection at the corner of the park. I checked for press plates. He didn't have them, but he did have his lights off and his windshield wipers going, which seemed a bit strange at 5:00 A.M. Who could this guy be waiting for in Gramercy Park?

It wasn't until I'd rounded the northwest corner of the park that I could make out, through the mist, that he'd stopped waiting. He'd started following us.

According to my FBI files, courtesy of the Freedom of Information Act, I've been tailed by professionals at least twice before: once by the Secret Service in Key Biscayne after I lightheartedly announced to the press room that I was inviting the Hell's Angels for a spin on Bebe Rebozo's yacht, the other time by the Weather Underground when I said something to make them suspect I was meeting with the FBI to betray some confidences we shared about the Timothy Leary breakout. I *was* meeting with the FBI, but only to demand they return the hunting knife they confiscated from my baggage on Air Force One.

All of which is by way of saying the strange guy in what looked like a forest-green Rolls who began tailing us as soon as my car pulled away from the curb was not a pro at the trade. Either that, or he didn't give a shit that he was making himself obvious by staying less than a car-length behind my aging Dodge.

Just to test my paranoia, always high after coming down from O, I drove around the whole of Gramercy Park, then stopped the car, got out and wiped the dew off the back windshield. The guy in the green limo made all four turns with me, then stopped and waited for me to get back in the car. In the early dawn light I could make out black hair and a blue blazer behind the wheel of the beautiful green machine. He ran the light at Twenty-second Street to follow me into Park Avenue.

"Listen, Lilah, I don't want to alarm you, but there's a man in a green Rolls-Royce trailing us. Could he be a friend of yours?"

She whirled around. "Oh, god. It's Victor," she sighed. "The creep. The stinking Ivy League pimp! And it's not a Rolls—it's a Bentley."

"You know him?"

"Lord, yes. Who *doesn't* know Victor, the literary pimp. Of course it's unfair to call him a pimp, the pimp. At Elaine's they call him the Introducer. He has a class act."

"Would you like to introduce me to him now, or would you like me to lose him?"

"You could do that?" she asked skeptically. "Pray tell Lilah how."

"We go visit the morgue. It's not far from here, over on First and Thirty-first. We go down the ramp to the underground parking on First Avenue. They'll let me in because of my NYP plates. Victor won't follow us in there because there'll be lots of cop cars flashing danger signals to him. The morgue guys there know me. I wrote them all up once—a piece on how they're the most psychically healthy people in the city—from their intimacy with death, you see . . . ."

"Listen, darling, this is fabulously interesting about the morgue and all, and I hope you'll send me a copy of that wonderful story, but how will we lose Victor? Won't he just wait for us to come out?"

"I was coming to that. We'll drive out the meat-wagon ramp. That opens onto the side street. You can get to it from the underground parking lot; the morgue guys will let me through. They'll think I'm doing it to impress a date, or something. I actually did once."

"I'm sure it was a divine evening, but tell me: I'm right in assuming that by 'meat wagon' . . . ."

"I mean the van that brings the corpses back from the death scene in the red rubber bags. Also, I got a friend there, helped me on a story—he works the meat-wagon night shift. A little weird, this guy, but he can give us the word on what the cops are looking for in Foster's death. It might turn out he actually worked on— Oh, I'm sorry. You were telling me about Victor."

"Oh, Victor. He's some character. The Introducer,

they call him at Elaine's. The story I hear is that he got his start back in 1960 as a JFK advance man. That was his title, but his real job was keeping the media sexually satisfied. Really. He'd go into a town ahead of the JFK campaign stop, line up some coeds—he was good-looking back then, just out of Princeton—tell them about the big-time reporters they could meet if they hung around a certain bar—usually in the hotel he'd book the press into. If he ran into trouble getting local talent, he'd call New York and fly in some light hooks, then lead the reporters to them. He'd pick up the tab for the hooks and ask them to pretend they were being seduced by these media guys. They loved it. Made them feel like real studs. Some of them never got over it.

"Later, the story goes, Victor moved up to become a kind of advance man for JFK himself—if you know what kind of advances I'm talking about. 'Road testing,' Victor called it, the creep."

I swung the Dodge north around the winding Vanderbilt Avenue ramp, then made a sharp U-turn around Grand Central and back downtown through the Park Avenue underpass, just to make sure Victor was serious about staying on our tail. He was.

"You have to give him credit for being a survivor," Lilah sighed. "It didn't take him too long after Camelot died to find Elaine's and discover he could still serve a function.

"The story goes that his first legendary introduction was when he secretly set up that meeting on the street outside Elaine's between Philip Roth and the woman who became "the Monkey" in *Portnoy's Complaint*. After that it was easy. You see, a lot of these big-name writers get lonely and horny sometimes, and they can't get laid or they can get it on only with lit-crowd groupies who don't provide them any good new material for their novels and who just as often turn around and write them up in *their* novels. Getting to be the same problem for women writers, these days.

"So a guy like Victor has a function. He hangs around Elaine's early in the evening, sees who's hunting, gets a sense of what they're after. Do they need a young, long-haired girl to figure in their next novel? He'll make some calls or visit some class singles bar or take a spin up to Briarcliff or Sarah Lawrence—depending on their taste, of course—and find just the right type, who's willing to be introduced to a writer. Famous writer walks out of Elaine's at closing time, Victor ushers him over to the Bentley. 'There's a woman sitting inside who's very eager to meet you,' he says. Writer finds compliant fantasy or good novel material within."

"You're not making this up?"

"I've seen him operate. Of course, some of his stories may be embroideries. Remember the John Leonard column about the big-deal middle-aged intellectual who showed up at a dinner party with a hot young bimbo? Victor claims that was his 'introduction.' The orgy scene in Erica Jong's last novel? Victor says he brought that sex therapist couple all the way from Sweden to make it work. And remember that great Woody Allen story, 'The Whore of Mensa,' about a madam who caters to the sexual fantasies of intellectuals? Victor claims it was based on his services."

I turned left on Thirtieth and headed over toward First Avenue and the morgue.

"So is that where he gets the money for his Bentley? Do these writers pay him?"

"Cash? No, not for women. All he asks for is the privilege of hanging out at the good table in Elaine's. No, he makes his cash from another kind of introduction. Maybe you remember a short story by one of the guys at the center table at Elaine's about how he and some writer friends got introduced to coke and found themselves a little hung up on it for a while? Fiction, of course. But I hear Victor was the introducer. A lot of big-money screenplays have been rushed out on Victor's coke.

"I've heard one hotshot literary agent say she had at least a dozen clients with outstanding advances in seven figures all begging for coke to meet the deadlines in their step deals. Natch, she turns to Victor. You could call Victor one of the great promoters of the filmic arts in America. However, I still call him a pimp."

"You had some dealings with him?" I asked.

"A while ago some of my partners and I had managed a tight corner of the Thai weed import routes, and Victor was looking to supply the 'Saturday Night Live' camp followers. I got to know Victor's scene for a while. It's ugly—he's a vicious, decadent swine beneath his English suits and blueblood charm. He's got a violent hair-trigger temper from a decade of Peruvian flake, and I had to stop him from pistol-whipping a friend of mine once."

"Why do you figure he's tailing you now? Could he know about you and Foster?"

"I don't know. Victor knows too many secrets for anybody's good. God, he makes me shudder. I'll take a morgue over Victor any day."

"You got it. We're here."

3

A TALK IN THE
BABY LOCKER

L et me tell you, the baby locker of the city morgue is no place to start feeling the black beast stirring. I'm talking about the wild-animal viciousness of a first-class opium hangover. When the black beast starts gnawing and twisting your innards, snarling and leaping with murderous paranoid rage against the inside of your rib cage, you want to be in a quiet place. You want gentle, muted lighting or maybe none at all, a pot of pitch-black, French market, chicory-laced coffee, and a good supply of Dramamine with the tablets already removed from the cursed plasticine bubbles they package them in, preferably administered with great tenderness by a young, attractive, licensed masseuse trained to soothe spasmodic muscles.

You don't want to be in a tiny room lined with dead babies in refrigerated file drawers, a room stinking with formaldehyde, blinking epileptically with the static buzzing of a faulty fluorescent, a room dominated by a six-foot-six, half-mad ex-neurosurgeon who now works the graveyard shift on the morgue wagon in order to explore some odd cabalistic theories he has about messages from God.

But that's the kind of room I was in when the heavy post-opium nausea hit. I had left Lilah impatiently sitting in my car, parked now in the underground garage of the morgue, while I sought out Saperstein, the morgue wagon man. Time was running out, Lilah reminded me when I left her. She had to get downtown and remove something she referred to only as "vitamins" before the police got there, or some other nameless people she seemed even more frightened of.

And Victor, the literary pimp who'd been following us in his green Bentley ever since Lilah dragged me out of my opium dream and into her crisis—how did she know he wouldn't tire of waiting outside for our car to reappear? Maybe he'd decide to risk the cop contact and cruise down the ramp after her.

It was worth the risk, I'd assured her, to see Saperstein. If he'd been on his schedule on morgue wagon shift tonight, Saperstein would have arrived at Elaine's to record the official condition of Walter Foster's body at death. It would be Saperstein who would wrap it in the red rubber body bag and drive it back to the morgue for pre-autopsy cooling in the storage room. Saperstein would know what the cops knew.

Naturally, I found him in his odd place of retreat and readiness.

"Shit," he said when I pushed the heavy door of the baby locker open. "You look like you're dyin', man. You want to cool off on a slab out there?"

"Why don't you stop molesting dead babies and take up an honest trade like proctology?" I suggested.

"I see enough assholes in here already," he replies, looking pointedly at me.

Funny guy, Saperstein. Funny weird as well as funny ha-ha. I got to know him when I was writing about the strange death of the twin podiatrists. And he'd decided to trust me—late one night in the baby locker—with the strange story of the voices that drove him out of brain surgery and into the morgue.

He began to hear the voices not long after he'd been promoted to the chief residency in neurosurgery at Massachusetts General. The night before a big operation, they'd waken him up, urgently, insistently, warning him: "You are not meant to cut into the living brain. You will understand."

Then one day in the operating room, as he began performing a routine lobotomy, he understood. As soon as he touched the razor's edge of his microtome scalpel to the exposed prefrontal lobe, some crazy circuit was completed somewhere; Saperstein suddenly began to feel, or imagine he felt, as if he were plunging his scalpel into his own cortex. He ran from the operating room clutching his head, screaming.

He never touched a scalpel again. Not to anything living. He became a morgue wagon man, his specialty the diagnosis of the D.O.A. And he was happy as a loon because the voices had returned, this time with a mission. They were telling him that the baby locker was a special place, that any time God permitted something so sad as the death of a newborn child, it had to be to call attention to an important *message*. But the messages weren't getting across, and the babies were dying in vain, the voices told Saperstein. His mission was to decipher the messages.

When I walked in, I found Saperstein trying to apply some cabalistic numerological formulas to the locker/slab numbers assigned each of the newly dead babies awaiting autopsy.

"Our newest guest is baby Nicholas," Saperstein told me after I'd closed the door. The baby locker is the only part of the morgue's huge basement storage cellar where the slabs—mini-slabs in this case—were closed off in their refrigerated file drawers in a separate room.

"Baby Nicholas, nicknamed Nick Alas, is in locker number 76," Saperstein said, pointing to a small drawer on the back wall. "Nick's 76. Nix Nick. Knock knock. Who's there? Not Nick. Seven and six are 13, the number of states in '76 at the birth of the American baby. One and three are four; the *Cabala* says of the holy number four that when the *sephirot* splintered into 288 sparks, four were set aside and—"

"Saperstein, please. I've got the new English translation of Isaac Luria's journals. I'll bring them to you, we'll talk 'breaking the vessels' for hours. Right now I need info. Walter Foster. Did you go up to Elaine's to get him?"

"Walter Foster. Prematurely gray. Whole body prematurely gray. High watt, soft white. Light bulb burnt out from the inside. I'd say his heart will weigh 350 grams, maybe more." Among the numbers that figure importantly in the abstruse calculations in the concatenations of which he hoped to find God's message, Saperstein took very seriously the metric weight of the heart, dutifully reported on the autopsy report before the organ is discarded.

I surpressed a formaldehyde-sated heave. "Saperstein, please, I need this info fast."

"Sorry. Yes, I was up there at Elaine's. Media circus already when I arrived. *National Enquirer,* *National Star* had flown in squads of Australian journalists. Fistfights like a rugby match. Precinct homicide guys can't control it, get any work done. Elaine ordering them around like they were waiters, when in walks Matchbook Dockery to take over the investigation."

"Matchbook, huh?".

Richard Dockery, aka "Matchbook" and "Hickory Dick," was the flamboyant homicide cop who headed an ad hoc flying squad within the department that was sometimes irreverently referred to as the "celebrity murder squad." The guys who handled the class A slayings with famous names, fortunes, and reputations among the dead or suspect. In the course of a 20-year vice squad and homicide career, Dockery's files on the doings and undoings of the socialites, politicians, and jet-set decadents had become an underground legend in Big Apple power circles.

A lot of powerful people owe him heavy favors: the senator netted in a routine raid on a gay bar and allowed after a plea to Dockery to be booked under a phony name, the publishing tycoon who was an insatiable client of a top-of-the-line, state-of-the-art-in-decadence madam who specialized in dominance and lashings, the high-level church official who had arranged regular delivery of angelic choir boys for initiation into the Platonic mysteries. Dockery had it all in his files. Consequently, a lot of people who didn't like him sucked up to him. He was not unlike Walter Foster in some ways.

"Anyway," continues Saperstein, "Dockery starts issuing orders and people. He's calling for a complete seating chart of the front room. Got two flunkies with clipboards taking notes on who's sitting where. This woman Elaine knows most of it by heart—who sat with whom and why; why these people used to sit together but never speak and why this guy hated Foster enough to swear once he'd tear his spleen out with his bare hands.

"I'm getting the body wrapped up in the rubber bag—crazed photographers won't let me close to it till they get one last shot of that seersucker suit—when Kiernan of the *Daily News* comes out of this other dining room everybody is calling Siberia with a glassine envelope filled with white powder.

"Well, all the reporters there groan and jeer. They figure this has got to be a plant by Matchbook. You know the story how he gets that name, right?"

Right. In his up-and-coming vice squad homicide career, Dockery wasn't above keeping himself at the forefront of the newspaper coverage of sensational slayings by carrying around a pocketful of matchbooks from gay bars and porno novelty shops he'd raided.

Say, he's at a murder scene and he's got no leads. Does he tell the reporters he's stumped, or does he maybe drop a matchbook from a gay bar behind a chair and then "discover" it and get a front page of the *Daily News* for himself: "HINT HOMO LINK IN E.

SIDE SLAYING"? Well, there were those who felt he did it, and that Kiernan, the grand old man of police reporters, wasn't above encouraging him. In fact, I've heard Kiernan is ghostwriting Dockery's autobiography for him.

"So anyway, plant or no plant, after the coke turns up, suddenly this bartender is real eager to talk to Dockery.

"They seem to know each other from when the guy was working Clarke's. I'm zipping up the body with Dockery watching when the bartender tells him he's got to talk to him in private, urgent.

"Dockery's launching into his tirade about no special treatment for anybody in his investigations, when the bartender says, 'What if I could tell you something about the woman in white and a man named Robert Letzgo?'"

"Dockery puts his arm around the guy, leads him into Siberia, empty now. That's all I know except Dockery's back here now with Kiernan. They want another look at the body for some reason, maybe just to see it without the seersucker suit on. It's worth seeing. That gray color is unnatural for a body only dead a couple hours. It's like he died a while before he was murdered, if you get what I mean."

I wasn't paying a hell of a lot of attention, I have to admit, because I'd begun hearing voices. Real ones, not Saperstein's kind. It was Dockery and Kiernan come to roll out the slab and take a look at Foster before the autopsy knife cut him open. I could hear them through the wall of the baby locker as Dockery slid out Foster's slab.

"So I can go with the Letzgo angle. Guarantee it page one for the Four-Star." That was Kiernan talking.

"You use any of that Letzgo stuff, I'll slit your throat on one of these slabs." That was Dockery. "And don't bullshit me. You got a lock on page one with the dope angle alone. Did the desk like 'SEEK DOPE DOLL IN EATERY SLAYING'?"

Dockery liked to pass on suggestions for headlines to the *Daily News* for some of the sensational slayings he'd been working on. Usually the *News* did better on their own. Then it hit me. Dope doll. Christ, they were talking about Lilah, who'd arrived at Elaine's with Foster, fled the scene after the shooting, and was sitting in my Dodge out in the underground garage not too many steps away. I had to get out of the baby locker and warn her, but I was trapped until Dockery and Kiernan finished with Foster's slab and left the coast clear.

"She seems like a pretty classy type to be involved in a heavy smuggling scene," Kiernan was saying.

"That's it," Dockery said. "Class. She built it up to a point where she wasn't selling dope. She was selling the advantages of class. She'd developed an all-woman network of totally reliable, nearly fail-safe dope couriers, all of them recruited from the same few Swiss prep schools—international travelers already, a sprinkling from Madeira. You know the kind of prep school I mean."

"Not exactly," says Kiernan. "My kids go to Vial of the Most Precious Blood Junior High. Are they something like that?"

"Don't break my balls, you get the idea. The biggest return on a dope deal investment goes to the person who finances the border crossing. I tell you the Customs inspectors did a total body search on Cardinal Cushing more times than they open these girls' pocketbooks. They have that look, you know. So this Lilah is a very smart executive too. She knows banking, Swiss banking. Offshore funds. The one thing her father tried to teach her, she paid attention to. This one advanced beyond smuggling to something just a little shy of a multinational corporation. Not bad for a West Texas prairie girl not yet 30. 'Course, she couldn't have done it without taking that poor Nicaraguan son of a bitch ex-husband of hers for a ride."

"This is the guy who's with Letzgo now?"

"Said to be operating under the title Consultant on Intergovernmental Relations, but as I understand it from the Feds, he's basically a lackey and a money launderer. She destroyed him. He used to be very big in the diplomatic pouch-smuggling game. Runs off and marries her. She pumps him dry of everything he knows. All his contacts. She gets him into heavier weight. Plane loads. Very tense high-level stuff. He starts making mistakes. Dangerous ones. Starts drinking, doing too much coke. She leaves him, his people follow her, he sells himself to Letzgo."

"How'd you get this so fast?" Kiernan asked Dockery.

"I just got off a long phone call. Had a long talk with a guy down in D.C., Investigator for the subcommittee that did the Letzgo hearings. He's got a lot of shit on the money people in that whole pirate king set. This is ten minutes after I get a call from this assistant counsel at the S.E.C. He hears on the 5:00 A.M. news about Foster, and tells me he got a low-key inquiry from a guy in the civil division of justice a few weeks ago asking what he knew about Letzgo's cash going into Horizon Lines Unlimited Ltd., an offshore tax-shelter venture that had been backing Foster's movie studio grab till the end."

"I could go with it now: 'LINK LETZGO TO MEDIA MURDER.' We could have it on the stands in an hour."

"No. I swear on my mother's slab I'll give it to you first if I nail it, but I can't afford a matchbook-type thing here. Know what I mean? Meanwhile, we can have a grand old time busting chops on some of our media friends."

"You think any of those literary nosepickers would have the balls to actually murder him?"

"Look, the way I understand it, half the people in the front room of Elaine's tonight have sworn to kill the guy in front of witnesses consisting mainly of the other half. I don't give a shit if they were half sloshed, if it was some metaphor or what shit they'll throw at me. I got a license to bust chops. If they don't make a voluntary statement, I'm walking them into a grand jury room, handing 'em immunity and squeezing 'em till the pus comes out."

"What I can't figure," says Kiernan, "is what it is about this guy Foster that he managed to make so many enemies. There weren't many people standing around weeping at Elaine's tonight."

There was a rumbling sound, Dockery rolling out the corpse of Foster on the slab. Then I heard steps coming down the corridor of body lockers.

"Inspector, sir." This was a new voice, thin and hesitant by contrast with the rough tones of the two men at the slab.

"Inspector, sir, if I might be permitted to interrupt you, I have those file cards on literary feuds I mentioned to you . . ."

"It's that twerp in the dinner jacket from up at Elaine's," Saperstein whispered to me.

"I think we can cross-reference them with the chart of people who were there tonight and—oh my god, is that . . . ?"

"This is his new table, sonny. He's got it all to himself, can't you see? And this is a very exclusive place. It's not easy to get a table here. The boys keep this row of slab cabinets reserved for my special cases."

"In the book I'm gonna call it the Celebrity Slab

Wall. The Inspector's like this Elaine dame—he don't let just anyone cool off here. Dorothy Kilgallen was up there in that corner, right Inspector? And that one over there was Joey Gallo. Up there was the woman who was—"

"Enough, enough, will you, Kiernan? Mr. St. George here is going to help break this case wide open with his filing cards, isn't that true, sonny?"

"Well, Inspector, I wouldn't presume to suggest that this information would have any value without your investigative talents; however, from a familiarity with the media world, I think that after I can outline for you the hostility vectors among the tables that night and we can correlate them with the ballistics evidence, I think we'll end up with that genre our friends the British love to call the closed-door mystery."

"Speak for yourself about friends when you're talking about the murdering redcoat torturers of Bogside and Derry," Kiernan advised.

"As you know, Lieutenant, in such cases the murder is committed in an enclosed space with a finite number of people present, each with motive, means, and opportunity for the murder."

"You telling me everyone in that card file wanted him dead? I know these literary feuds are bitter and vicious. But I can't take an annotated copy of the *New York Review of Books* into a grand jury and ask for murder one on the basis of some sneering parenthesis."

"Well, that's some exaggeration, but I think that in my card system here I have the most comprehensive cross-referenced chronicle of contemporary literary celebrity feuds available anywhere, and I think you will find that at virtually every table in the front room we can find a point of origin of what I like to call, for the purposes of our chart, a hostility vector.

"Hostility vector."

"It's hard to explain, but these literary feuds bear bitter fruit, Inspector. I've just limited my preliminary vector analysis to the 70's, but here you have five major magazine feuds alone where various people aren't speaking to each other, to Foster, or to their friends because of what Foster's *Media Confidential*'s 'Famous Feuds' section quoted or misquoted them as saying. And that doesn't begin to take into account the suspicions generated by Foster's famous serial. It gets very complicated, but I see you have a big chart with the table settings. Should we go back to your office? I brought some colored magic markers . . . ."

"You'll get used to it down here, sonny. It's just formaldehyde, not poison. Might encourage you to compress some of the details, get to the heart of the matter and all that if we stay down here. Why don't we just roll out slab Number 101 here and spread the chart out on it? The police artist boys have done a fine job with this seating chart, wouldn't you say?"

"You know what slab that is, Inspector," Kiernan

jumped in. "Wasn't that Amy Vanderbilt manners dame there, the one who jumped and—"

"Uh, Inspector, if I may." It was St. George again. "Before we go on. The information I've accumulated here is of no mean value to literary historians and, needless to say, has some sensationalist value to every common police-beat reporter in town. I feel that I would prefer to entrust the confidences and the conclusions I draw only to a properly constituted authority such as yourself, certainly not to someone who is at least arguably a rival journalist. And so, if Mr. Kiernan doesn't object—"

"You little Ivy League faggot you, trying to cut me out of this story with a bunch of index cards?"

I heard another rumble as another refrigerated slab compartment trundled out on the other side of the baby locker. There was a crackling of stiff paper.

"Okay, this is your north here, you've got your bar here, and then this square here is the big pillar in the front dining room. Silly as it seems, that pillar is a key to the seating dynamics. The well-trained maitre d' can use it to deflect eye contact between feuding parties. Right now, what I'll do roughly here is use separate colors for each faction in the various feuds. For instance, the first significant one of the 70's was the big *Harper's Magazine* split over the dismissal of Willie Morris. So we'll trace in red and green the hostility vectors still left over from that feud, like so. Needless to say, Inspector, I've got citations for each of these. Here, for instance, on the *Harper's* matter, is a quote from David Halberstam, who wrote that fabulous book on the war, *The Best and the Brightest*. I've got his faction in feud A drawn in red. According to Gael Greene, he hasn't quite forgiven Elaine for seating him at a table 'next to that miserable son of a bitch' from the green faction here. Next, we have the feud over *New York* magazine. Well, there were two of them. First, the founders' factional dispute between Breslin, Maas, and Hirsch on the one hand and Felker on the other, then, of course, the Murdoch/Felker thing; I've got the color codes for those on these cards. Then there are the more personal, the hatchet jobs on friends. I say we draw little hatchets into the stick figure's heads like so. Then there's the stolen story ideas and the stolen wives. Why not a flying dollar sign and a flying spouse sign here? You can see the complexity of the web of vectors, and when you factor in the squabbling over the way Foster reviewed the history of each feud in *Media Confidential . . .*"

"Inspector, this guy's nuts."

"Kiernan, it's not this guy. It's this world he's talking about. People get too much attention; they pay too much attention to themselves. But listen, sonny. Come to the point, we all know they hate each other's guts. Who did it to Foster?"

"Well, Inspector, I'm flattered you should ask because I could suggest a theory that may sound bizarre and literary at first but which might fit the situation in the absence of a critical mass of hostility vectors pointing to a single suspect."

"Cut the gibberish please, sonny," Dockery said, his feigned patience wearing thin.

"Well, I know it's presumptuous, but have you considered the Agatha Christie solution, Lieutenant?"

"She wasn't there, was she?"

"Actually, sir, she died herself—natural causes— some time ago. No, I mean the variation on the locked-room mystery she played upon in *Murder on the Orient Express*. Where each individual suspect appears to have a motive for the murder and the investigation is led astray by the search for one culprit, when in fact, *everyone of them* was in on it."

"Are you trying to say that the entire literary world conspired to murder this guy? Did they all have a finger on the trigger, or did they draw lots? You know any of them could shoot straight?"

"Perhaps not, sir. But as you might be aware, several of the top professional writers on organized crime, the Mafia writers' Mafia, hang out at Elaine's. Is it not conceivable that they could have made contact with a professional who could be brought in for the contract? Unlike literary people, these professionals are said to be able to maintain discreet silence about their work."

"Now wait a minute, aren't you forgetting something? One question."

"Sir?"

"Why now? Why go through with some elaborate contract now, when this guy Foster has been out of circulation for a couple of years. Sure, he pissed a lot of people off with his mags, but why bother getting him now?"

"Well, Lieutenant, have you considered the possibility that lately he hasn't been out of circulation, perhaps just out of sight. He never completed that scandalous serial about Elaine's he'd been publishing. Maybe he was going to revive it. Perhaps he's been engaged in some kind of new project that may have aroused the old hostilities. Perhaps you should check on his current contacts with them."

"Well, sonny, I appreciate your cooperation. Finish that chart and call my office tomorrow."

I heard the sound of the slab being rolled back and steps of the three men retreating. Saperstein stopped me before I got to the door to the baby locker.

"Before you go," he whispered urgently, "I need to ask you a question."

"Make it quick or, better, call me. My phone's been connected again. I gotta be somewhere fast."

"Just tell me this," said the huge morgue man, approaching me and detaining me with a powerful grip. "If I were to say to you, 'Steward, I will have some consommé,' would that mean anything to you?"

"Well, first of all, my name isn't Stuart, that's that twerp with the file cards, and you're hurting my shoulder, and I've got to go."

92

He didn't let go. "Steward, not Stuart. 'I want some consommé,'" he repeated, squeezing my shoulder to the point of pain.

"Okay, okay. I want some consommé. You mean the White House tapes, I guess. Every once in a while, during one of their coverup sessions with Haldeman and Ehrlichman, you hear Nixon buzzing his White House steward for some soup. He seemed to like the stuff a lot. What's it to you—you thinking of going to work as a White House steward?"

"Okay. The White House tapes, you say," he said. "Now one more question. You were down there in Washington during Watergate, what does 'Deep Six' mean?"

"Deep Six," I said. "How soon they forget. That's what Ehrlichman told Dean to do with the mysterious contents of E. Howard Hunt's safe before the FBI got to it. 'Deep Six them'—throw them six fathoms deep in the Potomac River. Dean eventually convinced old Pat Gray to burn whatever those documents were. Listen, Saperstein, I'm glad you've taken an interest in our nation's most profound constitutional crisis four years after it's over, and I'd be happy to sit down with you some time and return to yesteryear and tell you many amusing anecdotes about those stirring times. But I've got to run. Thanks for your help, old boy. Keep your hands off the warm bodies."

Time was not running out. It *was* out. Dockery's man had to have tracked Lilah's address by now and would be on the way to both places. I had to convince her it would be too dangerous to show up at either place. Especially if there were large quantities of illegal substances stashed within them as she'd hinted.

The lighting in the underground garage of the morgue is terrible. Some crooked contractor must have kicked back a fortune to unload these terminally defective, buzzing, flickering, fluorescent fuckers.

It wasn't until I was within a few yards of the car that I could make out it was empty. Lilah had gone.

4

FEAR IN THE FAN-TAN TUNNELS

There is something about the sight of a dozen dead ducks hanging by their beaks from a string that can cast a pall over your morning. I mean, just ten minutes earlier I'd skulked out of the morgue, which, all by itself, was enough to turn me into a vegetarian for life, and then I step out of a Checker at the corner of Mulberry and Canal and find myself face to face with a whole row of these damn ducks in the window of a Chinese grocery store that also featured a tank of appetizing live eels.

Sometimes at night the freshly barbecued birds can look mouth-watering in their crisp golden skins, although why the Chinatown guys feel they have to barbecue the whole duck—beak, eyes, and all, I don't know. In any case, this morning, in the 6:00 A.M. drizzle and steam of Chinatown smells, the ducks did not look mouth-watering. I did not like the way their necks had been stretched by hours of hanging over the fire, the glazed impassive look of their barbecued eyes. I did not share that tranquility. My stomach felt like a tankful of live eels.

Needless to say, I was not there on this fringe corner of Chinatown to savor the delightful ethnic diversity of downtown Manhattan. I was there because, about the time I discovered that my car wouldn't start and would have to be abandoned in the basement of the morgue, I had discovered a note left behind for me by Lilah on the front seat of the Dodge.

"Dearest One," it began. *"Join me at my Mah-Jongg place. Immediately please, darling. Mention Mel at the bar. Don't abandon me now.*

Yr. lady in distress & out of time."

Which was why I was on the fringe corner of Chinatown, staring at the dead ducks and gazing sideways at the weird neon-lit cocktail lounge next door, domain of Mel and other hot-shot illegal Mah-Jongg gamblers.

Now Mah-Jongg may not sound like a particularly threatening game to you, but when Lilah said Mah-Jongg in her note, she was not talking about little old Jewish ladies in rhinestone shades slapping tiles under beach umbrellas.

She was talking about a particular closely guarded illegal gambling parlor that operated in the backroom of that tacky-looking restaurant next door with a pink mock-Chinese neon script identified as "Henry Sing's Chinese American Bar-Grill."

Last time I'd seen Lilah in New York, she had pointed the place out to me on our way to a spicy but otherwise tame Szechuan meal. The game in the backroom was one of the most unique and exclusive illegal clubs in the aging ethnic casbahs below Canal Street, one of the few Chinatown rackets that permitted the patronage of select non-Orientals. It attracted, Lilah told me, a tough crowd of operators from the garment-center rackets, mainly older Jewish men who learned Mah-Jongg from their mothers at Bath Beach. They couldn't believe they could lose to the Chinamen at a game their own mothers played. It wasn't merely the dizzying dollar figures of the stakes at Henry Sings', but the stubborn ethnic pride of the players that gave the games the intensity of an intellectual Tong War.

I asked her how she knew all this. "A friend of mine in the sweater business imports a lot of alpaca from the Andes," she said. "Sometimes we do import deals together. He takes me there."

"How's the food?" I'd asked.

"Strictly speaking, there isn't any," she'd said. "You see, darling, people don't come here for the moo shoo pork. One reason they have those hideous pink neon pagodas out front is to discourage all you New Yorkers looking for your authentic little gems in Chinatown from even coming near. It's funny to watch when somebody actually does wander in for food. They shunt them off to an auxiliary dining room with about two tables, hand them a menu, and then call up Hong Fat and send out for whatever they order."

I glanced sideways at Henry Sing's blinking pink pagoda and then back to my friends the ducks. I knew I owed it to Lilah at least to warn her of what I knew the cops knew about her, but something about following her into Henry Sing's made me nervous. Not the idea of becoming an accessory after the fact, a trumped-up charge that certain parties know could never be made to stick by any honest prosecutor. Just the feeling that Lilah traveled with faster and meaner company than I felt like being introduced to this morning. After a good night's sleep and something to quiet the shakes coming on, I would be perfectly happy to follow her anywhere. But now, I stood looking at the barbecued birds thinking of poultry puns. I felt a need to exhaust them before taking action. Should I chicken out? Would that be ducking my responsibility? Was I a dumb cluck not to see the whole thing as a wild goose chase, fowl play, with poultry reward? If only I had a cape on. If only the Mod Squab were here.

That was enough. There's nothing like a bad pun sometimes to reach deep down inside to lance the abscess of self-loathing and make you want to reconstruct your self-respect.

When Lilah had been undraping and redraping her tanned limbs in the sweet warmth of my opium-fogged apartment it had been easy to be gallant. It would be easy to run out now, especially with that police car cruising down Mott Street toward me to inspire further paranoia. It would be easy, I could do it, as someone once said. But it would be wrong.

Do you know the way the foyers of most Chinatown restaurants are crammed with blowups of rave restaurant reviews framed behind cracked and yellowing glass—usually from obscure, frequently defunct neighborhood weeklies?

Henry Sing's Chinese American Bar-Grill hardly put up a show in this department. The glass door that led from the foyer to the interior had a lonely-looking review from a short-lived Upper West Side weekly in which I noticed the reviewer panned the hell out of the place. Something about the food having the "ineradicable taste of cardboard." Not the kind of thing to encourage the curious diner. I guess that was the point. The other plaque on the inner door displayed a clipping from a 1949 issue of the now extinct New York *Journal American*. It showed a stocky, muscular

Chinese gentleman shaking hands with then Mayor Bill O'Dwyer. This was not long before the mayor skipped town to Mexico in mid-administration to avoid talking to a grand jury.

The three guys sitting at the bar had their backs to me and didn't notice my entrance. Maybe it was the restaurant Muzak system which was turned up pretty high with the 101 strings playing "I Wanna Hold Your Hand" as I entered. Maybe it was the fact that the three of them, big, hefty garment-center "business-agent" types, were staring so raptly at the big color TV set over the bar.

I looked up at the screen. An attractive young woman in a black leotard was lying down, arching her back, and smiling engagingly as the show's logo, "Miss Debby's Let's Learn Yoga and Nutrition Show," floated across the screen.

In the red-flocked wallpaper and black Nauga-hyde padding of the barroom, cut off from the restaurant by one of those tacky beaded curtains, it was hard to remember that it was 6:30 in the morning, time for health nuts all over the city to rise and shine with Miss Debby.

The guys at the bar watching Miss Debby did not sound like health nuts. Miss Debby finished some warm-up exercises and began to do some intricate leg exercises that involved arching and stretching her body in a way not without interest to those who might be unconcerned with yoga.

"I tell you, Max. She's building up to The Plough today," said the guy in the houndstooth doubleknit. "I swear it. Remember the one I told you where the legs make this shape?" He tried to imitate a shape with his hands and knocked over a glass.

"Hey, Herbie, you can forget The Plough. Let me tell you about the one you missed yesterday where she rolls over into a headstand. You shoulda seen the squirrel shots, huh, Max."

"You can have her, you two," the one called Max said. "I like some tits on a woman. These yoga people have a law against tits or something?"

"Listen, Max," said the one called Herbie. "You ever see The Swan? I just want you to watch The Swan once. *Once*, you understand. Then I want to hear you talk tits to me."

"Maybe," said Max, "you should start talking money to Mort and me, Herbie. Remember, you signed some paper for last week's game."

"Uh, excuse me. I'm a friend of Mel's," I ventured.

"Who's Mel, sonny?" said the one called Max.

"You know," said Herbie, who seemed to have been drinking to cover his losses, "what we want is not a friend of Mel. If you had said you were a friend of Miss Debby up there you'd be telling us something. You ever run into her? Well, tell the uptight bitch she ought to answer her goddamn fan mail. Six-thirty in the morning she's on and already she's too busy to answer a respectful letter from a guy."

"I'm supposed to meet someone here, a friend of Mel's," I said.

"Herbie," Max barked out with some authority, "take your hand out of your pants and go find Mel."

"Ah hey, Max, don't make me go now when she's gonna do the goddamn Plough. It's the climax of a whole series of postures. I been waiting all week for this."

"Bad for your heart, Herbie, watching this every morning. Get Mel."

Herbie left his bar stool, giving Miss D. a smoldering look as she raised her legs into a headstand, giving me a vicious one as he smashed his way through the beaded curtains to the dining room.

By the time Herbie returned ten minutes later, Miss Debby had gotten up from the mat and, smiling blissfully, moved over to a blackboard for the nutritional segment of her show. Something about fiber. She wrote the words "internal transit time" on the blackboard.

Herbie punched his way back through the beads impatiently and glanced at the screen.

"Great," he said glumly, "I really was looking forward to this part of the show. Might as well turn to that old French lit broad on Sunrise Semester now, for all I care."

"You missed The Plough, Herbie," said Max cheerfully. "She said it was the climax of all that had gone before. But don't worry, it's only five minutes to Jane Pauley time.''

Herbie turned to me and jerked his thumb toward the curtain. "Mel says sit down and wait," he snarled.

The main dining room looked as if it hadn't seen a customer since the O'Dwyer administration. The field of white tablecloths dotted with the peaks of folded napkins crowning the place settings looked as if they hadn't seen an eggroll eaten in anger in ages.

At the far end of this forlorn field, however, there seemed to be some discreetly screened signs of life. Smoke and a muted mixture of chatter and the click of tiles drifted above some tall painted screens at the far end of the dining room. Then a head and shoulders appeared above one screen: a Chinese man dressed in the mustard-colored jacket and black bowtie of a waiter. Then the head ducked down and a minute later a big guy appeared at the side of one of the screens and headed toward me carrying a briefcase.

Mel was a big, powerful-looking guy, 300 pounds easily, and he was wearing a fairly bad toupee which made him look like George Steinbrenner.

"Mel's the name, Mah-Jongg's the game," Mel said, straddling the peeling black-lacquered chair opposite me. "Our mutual friend, the lovely lady from Texas, asked me to bring you this briefcase to look through while she attends to some business; she said there's a note inside, but say, listen, while I have you here, our friend Lilah says you're a member of the media, is that true?''

"Well, they don't give membership cards any more. I'm a writer for some magazines, or at least I used to be."

"Magazines. You know I read a lot of magazines. Regular media freak, you could say. See, I spend a lot of time sitting in guys' offices waiting for them to get out of conference so I can remind them of their financial obligations. So I have a lot of time for reading and I study the media. Kind of an unusual hobby for a guy in the garment center, but I read Liz Smith, Page Six, even take the *Columbia Journalism Review*, but I never really got a chance to sit down and chat with any of the media themselves like you here. I go for the inside stuff. I mean, this Rupert Murdoch—what's he really like? What's happening with the shake-up in the Washington bureau of the *Times*? Will Tom Snyder fire Jane Pauley if he takes over from Brokaw? And what's Bill Paley really up to in the news department, I mean after Salant retires? See, I'm not just talking about media hype, I'm talking about inside stuff. Maybe we could spend an evening together at Elaine's or something. You must hang out there, huh?''

God, I thought to myself. It's a plague, this media gossip—no one's immune. Aloud, I said, "I tell you

I'm not really an expert on that kind of thing, and I've never been to Elaine's, but I know just the guy who would love to talk to you about it. Very good friend of mine, name of St. George; you go up there and tell him Truman sent you and he'll talk your ear off. But tell me, where is Lilah?"

"Look, I know you're busy," he said. "But I'll give you a ring. Lilah gave me your number. She said she'll be out soon. There's some instructions she wrote for you in the briefcase. Fine woman, Lilah. See that you take care of her. Some of us feel very protective about her."

When Mel had returned to the games behind the screens, I unbuckled the old-fashioned clasps that bound the worn leather briefcase and found the following communication from Lilah on the back of a take-out menu:

> *Found these books and papers at Foster's place. Need to find out what he was up to with them to help clear me. Please figure them out while I finish some business with some investors.*
>
> *L.*

Inside the briefcase were some thick official-looking volumes and some file folders of loose papers. I recognized the official-looking beige paperbound volumes of House hearings and the green paper covers of Senate documents. Most of the volumes had torn, yellow place marks scattered through their thicknesses. The top folder had "Operation Night Manager misc. memos" scrawled across the front.

I picked up the big beige volume that lay underneath the folder of memos. It was entitled, "INQUIRY INTO THE ALLEGED INVOLVEMENT OF THE CENTRAL INTELLIGENCE AGENCY IN THE WATERGATE AND ELLSBERG MATTERS, HEARINGS BEFORE THE SPECIAL SUBCOMMITTEE ON INTELLIGENCE OF THE COMMITTEE ON ARMED SERVICES HOUSE OF REPRESENTATIVES NINETY-FOURTH CONGRESS."

I opened to the page marked by the yellow scrap of paper, page 1103. I glanced over the closely printed transcript of testimony. Mr. Nedzi, the Chairman of the Special Committee on Intelligence, was questioning a witness identified as Mr. Bennett about E. Howard Hunt, whether the CIA ordered Hunt's secret investigation of Chappaquiddick rumors in the summer of 1971.

Now this Mr. Bennett, I realized, as will all more-than-casual followers of unsolved Watergate mysteries, is none other than Robert F. Bennett, the man who hired E. Howard Hunt after Hunt "retired" from the CIA and while he was engaged in his dirty tricks work for the White House Plumbers. And this Mr. Bennett has also been identified by J. Anthony Lukas and other investigative reporters as a likely candidate for the real person behind the legendary "Deep Throat" who helped Woodward and Bernstein crack the Watergate case. Other investigators have identified Bennett as a part-time operative for the CIA who reported back to his case officer on the activities of both the Colsons and Hunts of the White House *and* the Woodwards and Bernsteins of the *Washington Post,* both of which groups of antagonists were his confidants. I looked more closely at the circled passage of his testimony on page 1103:

> MR. BENNETT: Howard came to me to say that it was Chuck's idea that he engage in an investigation of Senator Kennedy and did I know of any place where he might go to conduct such an investigation? I said Yes. As a matter of fact, having worked for Secretary Volpe, I know a lot of people from Massachusetts one of whom has always been disappointed that nobody ever asked him everything that he knows about the Kennedys, that he used to be the night manager in a hotel where the Kennedys used to come. He said he knew all about the Kennedys and that you might get something by interviewing him.

The only other mark that had been made on page 1103 was drawn with a heavy felt-tip pen under two words within that encircled passage. The two underlined words were: *night manager.*

The next three volumes were similarly place-marked, with passages circled and occasionally underlined. There was a copy of the White House tapes opened to a February 28, 1973, Oval Office talk between the President and John Dean with, again, a conversation about Kennedy and Chappaquiddick prominently marked:

P: If he would get Kennedy into it too, I would be a little more pleased.

D: Let me tell you something that lurks at the bottom of this whole thing . . . right after Chappaquiddick somebody was put up there to start observing . . . . He was there for every second of Chappaquiddick, for a year, and for almost two years he worked for Jack Caulfield.

P: *(Unintelligible)*

D: If they get to it—that is going to come out and this whole thing can turn around on that. If Kennedy knew the bear trap he was walking into—

P: How do we . . . Why don't we get it out anyway?

D: Well, we have sort of saved it.

Here, the words "bear trap" and "we have sort of saved it" were underlined heavily. I looked up across the dining room, but there was no sign of Lilah, just the sound of tiles and an occasional loud declaration like "four crack, two bam" and other unintelligible Mah-Jongg terms. I continued reading.

The next volume, a Congressional quarterly chronological account of the development of the Watergate scandal, was marked at page 243 and, under the heading August 1, 1973, the following passage was circled:

> KOPECHNE PROBE: White House aides ordered secret inquiries into the 1969 party at Chappaquiddick, Mass., and the subsequent car accident involving Sen. Edward M. Kennedy and Mary Jo Kopechne. Sources told the *Washington Post* that Anthony T. Ulasiewicz, a former White House secret investigator, authorized by Haldeman and John D. Ehrlichman, concocted a plan to lure friends of Kopechne to a New York apartment, seduce and secretly photograph them to gain information by blackmail.

The final official volume was a House Judiciary Committee's Impeachment Inquiry volume entitled "Pre-1972 Campaign Surveillance Activities, Volume II." Here there were two circled excerpts on the same subject. One was from the Senate testimony of John Dean, June 25, 1973, cited as "3 ssc 922–23":

> During the summer of 1969 while I was working at the Justice Department, the Deputy Attorney General Richard Kleindienst called me into his office and told me that the White

House wanted some very important information. Mr. Kleindienst instructed me to call Mr.
De Loach, Deputy Director of the FBI, and
obtain from him information regarding the
foreign travels of Mary Jo Kopechne. To this
day, I can only speculate that I was asked to
convey the information so that others could
deny they had done so, should the matter
become known.

In the same volume, on the page following Dean's
testimony, there was an excerpt from the Senate testimony of Haldeman aide Gordon Strachan with the
following phrases underlined:

. . . surveillance of Sen. Kennedy . . . And we
would, in fact, receive reports prepared by the
individual who was presumably reporting on
Senator Kennedy's activities . . . As you un-
doubtedly discovered or know, the incredible
interest in Kennedy the whole time I was there,
constant. I don't care what Kennedy said about
what his candidacy was or was not going to
be . . .

After going through all these government documents, I was surprised to find a commercial book at
the bottom of the stack. A black bound volume of E.
Howard Hunt's post-Watergate autobiography, *Un-
dercover*. Two pages in the Hunt book contained the
most curious story, the most extensive markings of any
of the government documents, and for the first time

some extensive annotations written in, what I suspected, might be Walter Foster's hand.

The circled excerpt began on page 208 and consisted mainly of Hunt quoting his partner, Plumber G. Gordon Liddy, after Liddy had returned from an inspection tour of a strange operation run by a rival New York branch of the Nixon secret operative apparatus.

> There seems to be some weird parallel operation going on up in New York. Caulfield—that gumshoe of Mitchell's—seems to be in charge and they've told me to go up and take a look at it . . . Something about one of the broads who was at the Chappaquiddick party—you know, one of the survivors. I gather they've set up some sort of fabulous pad and it's run by another ex-New York cop. The idea seems to be to have the broad fall in love with the ex-cop and while they're in bed together, automatic cameras are supposed to whir and buzz like *From Russia with Love* . . . .

Hunt continues:

> When Liddy returned from his New York inspection he telephoned me, and we met. Shaking his head and laughing, Liddy said, "The setup's unbelievable. This middle-aged guy who's in charge of the operation has an accent I can't place. And the pad! It's got to be

a cop's idea of an East Side bordello in the
1880's, second-hand furniture, red plush sofas
and the Golden Greek's trying to build a fake
wall—a partition—so he can get cameras behind it." Liddy laughed uproariously.

"I can just see him making out up there.
The gal takes one look at the pad and shrieks
for help. That's how subtle it is. And the
dough they're spending on it! I don't know
who the hell's idea it was but here was the
Golden Greek pounding up this great partition all day long and dating the broad at night.
My guess is that broad'll be finished with the
Golden Greek before he's finished with the
wall . . . . For a month down here I've been
thinking the Golden Greek had a great seduction setup in New York and once the broad was
compromised she'd tell the true story about
what happened that night at Chappaquiddick.
The Greek hasn't been getting very far with her
. . . ."

Later Hunt concludes:

I heard that the seduction suite had been
dismantled and the Greek* directed to other
pursuits.

It was the asterisk in this passage after "Greek" that
had drawn the most attention from the felt-tipped
annotator. The asterisk referred to the following footnote which was circled in red at the bottom of page
209:

*Not until the Ervin Committee televised hear-
ings was I able to identify New York police-
man Anthony Ulasciewicz as Liddy's Golden
Greek . . . .

Next to the encircled footnote, in bold-red printed
capital letters, the annotator had written the following:

No! Tony U. not the 'Greek.'

Then an arrow went up from this comment to the
phrase "the seduction suite dismantled" and the following was written in the margin:

*Misinfo—or disinfo to cover for Night Man-
ager? See section IIA in N.M. Memo.*

Well, this was getting interesting. Foster, or
whoever it was, seemed to have some alternate version
from Hunt's of the fate of this weird plan. I found the
folder marked "N.M. Memo" and, inside, a ten-page
document that was markedly different from those I'd
just read.

It was not, like the others, a document reprinted
in some public volume. It appeared to be an original
of some sort, bound in glassine, stamped "Confid./No
Dist." on a title page that read:

OPERATION NIGHT MANAGER. A PROPOSAL FOR
TRANSFER OF OFFENSIVE INTELLIGENCE CAPA-
BILITIES PREVIOUSLY UTILIZED IN OPERATION
GOLDEN GREEK.

I turned to the second page and found a table of contents with five items:

I   Assessment of Failure of Golden Greek Operation; the Need for Experienced Professionals

II   Damage Limitation: The Need to Create the Close-Down Illusion Among Golden Greek Principals, Possibility of Awareness by Adverse Forces in the Intelligence Community with Special Reference to Intertel/ Kennedy Complex

III Capability Assessment of Assets in Place

IV Targets of Opportunity and Strategic Value to RN Effort

V   Night Manager: An Action Option for Retargeting

I flipped to the last section, recalling the underlined reference to "Night Manager" in the first document, but before I could begin the "Action Option" section, Mel reappeared.

"You reporters. You guys. Always digging into documents, huh. The old Woodward and Bernstein routine. Lilah says you've got lots of stories to tell me— they're your close friends and all. Hey, what do you think about Barry Diller and Dick Snyder? I mean, is there a potential power struggle there? But don't worry, we can get into all that over dinner, maybe you can introduce me, but actually," Mel changed tone and looked a little apologetic, "we may have a bit of a security problem here that will require your packing up and leaving by the downstairs exit."

"Security problem," I said, stomach tightening. "What downstairs exit? What's going on? Where's Lilah?"

"Here, darling. Pack up your schoolbooks and follow me."

She was still wearing my clothes when she appeared around the screen and approached Mel and me, who were now standing, stuffing papers into the battered leather valise.

"There seems to be some unusual police activity out front. This game, of course, is well paid off with all the right people, but something seems to be going on outside that is causing my friend Mr. Sing some concern."

She took my hand and led me toward the screens at the rear of the room. "We're going to leave by way of some tunnels that will take us out the other side of Chinatown. We may be asked to take separate paths. Mr. Sing has guides for each of us. I know this is all mysterious, but it's even more urgent now I get to that apartment I told you about on Sullivan Street, the one across from Bob Dylan's old place. Here, take this key and meet me there. I need to know what you think of all those documents. You are wonderful, darling.

Behind that bumbling and confused façade, you are a true chevalier."

I'd heard stories of the legendary network of tunnels said to honeycomb the subbasements beneath the streets of Chinatown. An old police reporter I knew claimed to have gone on a police vice-squad raid in the late Forties that had penetrated a labyrinth that led from beneath a pawnshop on Pell Street and wandered for nearly a mile before terminating in a basement underneath a tallis factory on East Broadway.

Originally built almost a century ago to transport illegal Chinese immigrants and black-market items from the port to the safety of Chinatown without official interference, the tunnels had been expanded and maintained to serve as haven and escape route for a number of rackets, the most recent and popular being illegal gambling on fan-tan, a mysterious Chinese card game closed to Westerners.

Mel led me through a rusting kitchen area, through a broom closet in the rear of the restaurant, and down a rickety backstairs to a cellar. Herbie, Max, and a friend climbed down after us. Then down a further set of stairs to a narrow dirt-floored tunnel illuminated by an occasional Chinese lantern.

I smelled dank vegetation ahead, and as soon as we turned the corner into a broader plank-floored corridor, we found our path lined with row after row of beansprout planters and mushroom frames.

"Look, Herbie," I heard Max behind me, "sprouts

and mushrooms. If you'd been paying attention to the nutrition segment of Miss Debby's show, you wouldn't be screwing up your face in disgust like that."

Ahead of me, Mel said, "I can't understand those guys hooked on the yoga show. So, her leotard's a size or two too small and it looks good. But I go for the more serious women in the media myself. It's my opinion that NBC was crazy to let Cassie Mackin go to ABC. I mean, she's certainly a superior news reporter, and the fact that she's attractive shouldn't be a barrier. But you must know a lot about the internal politics of these network decisions. I mean, if Fred Silverman had been there at NBC would she be gone? And by the way, what was the story with 20/20, since we're talking about the TV news game."

There was no stopping Mel's media mania, even among the mung beans and mushrooms in the fan-tan tunnels of Chinatown. We came to another intersection. In the lantern light to the left, I could see figures moving and hear some excited conversation in Chinese. Mel was asking me whether I thought *Us* magazine was "pursuing a strategy of going after a more upscale audience *vis à vis People*, or whether there had been a conceptual change since the new staff had moved in."

It didn't seem to matter to him that I didn't have any answers to give him. He was in love with his idea of media sophistication for its own sake.

Several figures beckoned us through what must have been a hastily cleaned-up fan-tan parlor, and pointed to a ladder. We found ourselves in another basement where the waiter who peered over the screen back at Henry Sing's ushered us onto a mid-sidewalk cargo lift, switched on a motor and sent us creaking and groaning up toward the metal lift cover which opened to the sky above us. We were six blocks away from Henry Sing's on a quiet street opposite a park on the fringe of Chinatown. As we emerged, Mel was speculating about "the programming savvy of a Chancellor-Brokaw slot switch" and asking me if I could introduce him to Fred Silverman because he had some programming theories he'd worked out. I told Mel I'd do it the very next time I met the guy.

Twenty minutes later I had the cab let me off across the street from Bob Dylan's house. It was a very special block known as MacDougal-Sullivan Gardens. The houses that formed the four sides of the block enclosed a hollow square with one of the largest and most beautifully landscaped gardens in New York. It was not free, this internal Eden. It cost $1,000 per year for garden privileges. He paid. She paid. Her apartment was a spacious floor-through fronting on Houston Street, with a rear porch that was diagonally across from his entrance to the garden—the door to his laundry room. Don't ask me what it means.

I was too paranoid to think. I didn't want to round the corner and enter her apartment in plain view of whatever cops and thugs might be looking for Lilah. But the only alternative was to call up Dylan and ask him to let me go through the garden and into Lilah's by way of the back porch.

So here I am, trying to figure out which goddamn key fits the outer lock of her front door, when a cop car comes cruising toward me from the east. It passes slowly. I get the door open, but I don't know whether the cop's stopped. No way I can back out now. Up to the second floor and fast. Into the apartment, I set up the police lock.

Dust. The place looks like it hasn't been slept in since 1969. A thick wall-to-wall carpet of dust. It looked like a late Sixties place preserved untouched. Rich Indian silk hangings draped with filaments of dust. A path through the dust, recent it seemed, led into the living room. Big dust-covered silken pillows and musty Oriental tapestries hung with cobwebs. In the middle of the floor a big, glossy, brown Bendel's shopping bag, obviously brand new. Inside the bag was a box wrapped in tissue. "Vita Pet Doggie Vitamins" the label read. It was heavy—I'd estimate about two kilos worth.

I was unwrapping when I heard the sound from behind the swinging double door that led into the kitchen. Like a drawer opening. Then footsteps. I tried to set the bag down as noiselessly as possible and retreated toward the bedroom with a vague intention of hiding under the bed. Then someone kicked the swinging door open and I saw the flash of gun metal.

KIDNAPPED
IN A BENTLEY

The last time I had a gun pointed at me was back in '72—that insane incident at the Nixon family boathouse on Key Biscayne. I'd been down there covering the Republican National Convention, and the Secret Service somehow got the notion I was plotting to steal Bebe Rebozo's yacht.

They were wrong, of course. I never meant to keep it. I planned to bring it right back. As I explained to the humorless Secret Service guy who stuck a gun in my ribs the minute I set foot on the dock, all I wanted to do was take it out for a quick spin in the Bermuda Triangle after a stop-off in Haiti to pick up a highly respected voodoo exorcist. I had been consumer-testing mescaline in the Boom Boom Room of the Fontaine-bleau Hotel and decided to explore a theory a writer friend of mine had developed. He had the notion that some spirit from out of the Bermuda Triangle had demonically possessed Rebozo's boat while Nixon was aboard, causing the President to behave strangely thereafter. I told the Secret Service guy on the dock that he'd be making a substantial contribution to national security if he'd take his gun out of my belly and help this Haitian holy man to do voodoo ju-ju to Bebe-baby's boat.

The guy did put his gun away. He smiled at me and started whispering into one of those little wrist radios they have. I heard him use the word *strait-jacket.*

But facing this gun here in this strange, dust-choked, silken mausoleum of an apartment, I realized that any explanation I could give of what I was doing here wouldn't sound much more convincing than the one about the voodoo exorcist.

I would have to tell whoever was on the other end of that gun that a beautiful woman had awakened me from an opium dream around 4:00 A.M. this morning and told me she was wanted for murder and needed my help; that she needed me to accompany her to this apartment to pick up a Henri Bendel's shopping bag filled with a carefully wrapped package, of "doggie vitamins," she said, although she warned me not to feed them to a dog. Then I'd have to add that the woman disappeared while I was trapped eavesdropping on some homicide cops in the baby locker of the city morgue, a detour I'd taken when we'd discovered our car was being tailed by a green Bentley limousine driven by a strange character she referred to as "Victor, the literary pimp." Face it, I didn't believe that story myself and it happened to me.

So instead I decided on a more basic posture toward the gun facing me. You could call it a deep cringe.

"Don't shoot! Disabled vet!" I cried out. "Shrapnel tore out my spleen at Khe Sahn. For godsakes don't finish me off."

This gambit turned out to be fairly humiliating when Lilah herself emerged from behind the door, holding the gun and choking with laughter.

"What's so funny? Maybe I didn't lose my spleen, but the sight of a gun makes my heart murmur sound like a goddamn jackhammer. What's the idea disappearing and then sneaking up on me?"

"Oh, my errant knight," she exclaimed, dancing over and squeezing against me with what felt like real eagerness.

"I knew you would come through," she said,

disengaging herself from the embrace. "I didn't mean to scare you with this gun, but it could have been Victor or one of his girl thugs."

"You seem to have a lot of weapons at your disposal, but I suppose in your line of business . . . Listen, Lilah, the cops have got leads on who you are. They're gonna track this place down. Why don't you pack up whatever you're taking and we'll get ourselves some breakfast, call a lawyer, and decide what to do."

"Nobody," she said in a strange tone of voice, "will find any connection between this place and me. Only two people could know I'm here, and Victor is the only one I know who is looking."

"Why wait here for him to find you?"

"I'm not waiting. Until you came I've been look-ing for a safe-deposit-box key. It was supposed to be left for me here. Maybe it wasn't, maybe it was hidden, but I can't take the chance of anyone else finding it."

She picked up one of the cobweb-laced silken pillows from a low-slung divan. A billowing pillar of dust arose from the touch. Through the imprint of her hand, a few gleams of what had once been a gold-embroidered surface could be glimpsed. Lilah looked up at me, her cheeks and forehead smudged with charcoal grime, green eyes glowing in the dusky set-ting.

"Are you gonna get to work, or are you going to stand around and supervise?"

"I think I'll stand around and supervise," I said.

"Start with the dining-room table, and by the way, darling, what do you make of that homework I gave you to look over?" she asked.

"Lilah, I suspect you know as much or more than I could figure out from those documents. But I'll play along. I get the feeling Foster or someone he knew was trying to track down this Boiler Room Girls blackmail scheme because of the Kennedy angle. When he came upon some new twist to it that hadn't come to light—"

"A new twist?"

"Well, I'd like to know what exactly this 'Operation Night Manager' was and how far it got. All there was in that briefcase was a memo proposing it."

"I'd like to find that out too, darling. But first I need to find that key. Perhaps they'll be one and the same discovery. Attend please, dear one, to the dining-room table. Who knows where the bastard may have hidden it."

It was set for two. Good silver, once upon a time. A silver bowl that looked as if it might have held fruit and nuts, now filled with an aged and torpid fungus. Burnt-out islands of candle stumps poked through the foam of dust that rolled over what had once been a sea of damask.

"You know something, Lilah," I called to her in the living room, where I could see her pulling up carpets. "Dockery, the homicide cop, said you were a very tough business lady. Too tough for some of the toughest sharks in the Caribbean including your ex-husband, if he is ex. Now I'm not a tough shark, just a naïve, small-town boy who's easily misled by attractive ladies. I'm perfectly willing to be used and discarded. But will you please tell me just what the fuck this weird place is and what we're doing here?"

"A close friend of mine went out of her mind and tried to kill herself here. Satisfied?"

She'd finished searching the divan. Angry volcanic masses of dust rose into the air as she threw down the comforter off the majestic brass bed that dominated the sleeping alcove. The white sheets uncovered beneath were, momentarily, the only unsmirched surfaces in the place. Then the dust descended on them too.

"All right," she answered at last. "If you can stand hearing a very, very sad story, and you keep your precious ass moving till you find that key for me, I'll tell you."

She ripped the sheets off the mattress. "Seven years ago somebody played a vicious practical joke on my friend. You'd have to know her to know how devastating it was . . ."

At that time, in the sunset glow of the Sixties, a woman who was considered "magical" in a special way and who didn't have to worry about money could exist for her ethereal aura alone, floating through fashionable and unfashionable slums and salons, living on the luminescence of her very presence, although occasional supplements of soft psychedelics were required, like cosmetics, to rekindle from within the surface glow.

She was a "magic lady," Lilah's friend, the closest thing the Sixties had to the storybook princess of her childhood. And she might have continued this blissful dream life had she not succumbed to the sickness that her rarefied sort of royalty was more vulnerable to than most. Falling in love with a god. The more inaccessible the better. For some magic ladies it was Swami Uptown or Swami Downtown, at whose chastity they chafed.

For her it was an inspired, self-destructive, acid-poet rock star who decided he was a divinity incarnate as "The Lizard King," which is what he took to calling himself in his final days. You might recall him. His name was Jim Morrison. He had a group called "The Doors."

Lilah shoved the mattress off the bed and started searching among the rusted, creaking bedsprings for the missing key.

They'd never been introduced, never spoken. But somehow Lilah's friend knew, she just *knew*, that she was meant to mate with the Lizard King. Their paths had crossed just once, momentarily, at a crowded party, one of his last public appearances.

Unfortunately, she had taken MDA before the party. Do you remember that drug? The "love drug," they called it. God, the clumsy 'lude freaks who call their crude chemical the "love drug" will never understand the secret communion of MDA lovers. In a flash Lilah's friend decided her love was powerful enough to spellbind him and redeem him. To work her magic she needed just one night alone with him.

Of course, thousands of women probably felt the same way at one time or another. But not long after, someone appeared and offered this woman a chance to make it all come true.

He was an aspiring rock writer, the smooth-talking, sincere, laid-back type who had mastered the delicate art of mellow name-dropping, through which he hinted buddylike intimacy with certain godlike figures. So one day this writer visits Lilah's friend and after some solemn preliminary smoking he begins telling her in his most righteous tones:

"This is like a very, very heavy thing for me to say, but like, *he* told me he felt a very powerful vibe between the two of you at that party. He's been telling some people he trusts that he's about to embark on like the terminal stage of this Lizard King trip, and he needs like a final union, he was calling it, with a kindred spirit, and he said something like in another lifetime you two had been— Whatever, he's like a shy and weirdly circumspect guy and he's asked me to ask you if I could, like, help him work out whatever karma is between you two. He says the night of the next new moon is what the charts say is best."

He worked very fast, this writer. Before a week was out he had an apartment rented. This apartment. The porch in the back overlooks a beautiful interior garden. According to the writer, his "friend" had said that the vibes would be right for him to climb up to the back porch, which forms a sort of balcony over the garden, and come to her on the night of the next new moon. She was to put a lighted candle in the window overlooking the balcony that night to signal her readiness.

The poor woman spent the next two weeks half mad with ecstasy and anticipation and half exhausted from frantically trying to transform the apartment into a silken Persian bower of bliss, beautiful enough to enchant him for not one but a thousand and one nights. In addition to the candle for the balcony window, she filled the place with scores of candles and dozens of mirrors to multiply them into millions of glowing reflections.

As the sun went down on the night of the new moon, she took one tab of exquisite MDA, lit candles, and began to await the summons from the balcony. She waited all night. The MDA came on. The candles burned down. The Lizard King did not appear. The writer's phone didn't answer. The next night she waited with just one candle in the window. She woke to the sound of the garbage trucks outside inaugurating the new morning, and suddenly she knew she'd been taken. A week later they had to drag her out of the place in a catatonic stupor. She'd taken an overdose of MDA and she'd blown out certain circuits. Three weeks later, Jim Morrison died in Paris.

"What happened to her?" I asked Lilah.

"After they released her from supervised care she left for the Caribbean and became a different person."

"And this place? Don't tell me . . ."

"She became a different person, a tough person, but some crazy sentimental streak in her believed all those mysterious rumors that he wasn't dead and it wasn't his body they found in that bathtub in Paris. She had her trust fund maintain ownership under another name and gave orders to have the whole floor sealed up."

"Goddamn. Like Miss Havisham," I said.

"Who?"

"Have-a-sham," I said. "You remember, in *Great Expectations*—the old woman who spent half a century living in the decay of her wedding feast after the bridegroom didn't show."

"Oh. Yes," she said. "The writer who carried out the scheme made that comparison. He wrote up the whole thing, of course. Called it 'The Woman Who Still Waits for The Lizard King.' Leaving out his part in the affair, the story made a terrific lead anecdote for a story he was doing on the death of the Sixties. Walter Foster liked it so much he put it on the cover, complete with a whole Gothic-romance illustration of that night. As a matter of fact, the whole thing started at some late-night gathering at Foster's table at Elaine's.

He just tossed out the idea of the hoax as a perfect way to ridicule the pathetic devotees of a fake god, and this writer-toady slunk off to execute it. That's what I heard."

"God, you'd think this woman would arrange to execute *him*."

"Would you? Well, like I said, she became a different person down in the Caribbean." She gave up on the bedsprings and began tearing the tapestries down from the walls. "But what I didn't say was, maybe you've already guessed. I'm that different person. It didn't all happen to a friend, it all happened to me."

"My god. You." Suddenly an awful but obvious thought hit me. "Then last night at Elaine's. . . . Was it you—?"

"Did I kill Walter Foster? I've already assured you I didn't. We've taken a thousand mikes of Sandoz together, darling. You know I can't lie to you. Come, do you want to look into my eyes?"

They were wide open, moist, and very, very green. Oceanic in their depth. I took the plunge. When the horrid hacking buzzer broke the silence I was still at sea. It was, perhaps, the first time since *that* night that the buzzer had sounded. This was no bell-toned buzzer to start out with, but the years of disuse had since rotted the circuits so that it could produce little more than a throttled asthmatic death rattle. Then it stopped.

That could mean the party or parties had given up

and gone off. Or that they'd cracked open the flimsy outside door and were heading up here right now.

Lilah turned the gun on me. "All right, don't argue with me and don't pretend to be brave. Here," she picked up the Henri Bendel bag with the still-wrapped packages of the mysterious doggie vitamins and pushed them into my arms. "Take these. It's an easy jump down from the back porch into the garden. Head for the big apple tree and turn left. Look for a green door into a laundry room. Put these in a subway locker and wait at home to be contacted. Feed the dog. You've been wonderful." She kissed me forcefully.

"But you're not going to stay?" I began.

"I know what I'm doing." She leveled the gun at me. "Get your ass out of here."

Outside at last. Across the street, the brightening early-morning sun was stirring a derelict in the door-way next to Tiro A. Segno, the Italian rifle club. I didn't look like much of an improvement on him, it occurred to me. As I passed the Café Dante, I thought seriously about the hellish way I was leading my life. After this is over I'm going to have me some peace and quiet. Build me a cabin in Utah. I was humming to myself, while rounding the corner dominated by the sobering stucco structure of the James B. Rosso Mortu-ary Establishment.

"Psst." It was a summons from the pillar-sheltered niche at the entrance to the parlor. "Hey, come here." In the shadows, framed in the oaken door beneath the word *Mortician,* there beckoned a breath-taking vision.

She couldn't have been a few minutes older than the age of consent, and yet she looked as if she'd stepped out of another decade entirely. Lean and golden-limbed, with long, straight blond hair falling abundantly below her waist and a glow of sensual bliss lighting up her meltingly sweet eyes, she looked as if she had just been transported out of San Francisco's Golden Gate Park on that morning in 1967 when the best chemists in the Western world began giving away Orange Sunshine. She even wore—I swear to God—a flower in her hair. In her embroidered denim cutoffs, bare midriff and filmy, translucent tie-dyed top, she was a perfect, indeed too perfect, specimen of the extinct species once known as Flower Child.

The thing that spoiled the picture was the squat black gun she held in her hand.

"Hi," she murmured, smiling ever so sweetly, "my name is Laurel. What's your sign?"

"Gee, sorry," I said, "don't really believe in astrology, got to get going. Nice—"

"Listen, Bozo," she hissed, "I don't got all day. Get over here and tell me your fucking sign or I'll blow a hole in your intestines."

"Well, uh, Sagittarius, but I mean what—?"

"Oh, wow, a Sag," she said. And suddenly she was a smiling, mellow-voiced psychedelic princess again. "I can see in your chart that you're about to walk quietly around the corner and get into a big green car and meet some nice people who want you to help them out with some information. I can also see in your chart that if you try to get away a bullet is going to sever your spinal cord and you'll piss in plastic bags the rest of your life." She smiled sweetly again. "I'm a Libra myself, although my moon's in Sagittarius. Now, start walking."

There it was. As I turned the corner and headed west toward Sixth Avenue, I saw the long, sleek green Bentley—the one I'd thought I'd left behind at the morgue—glide up to the curb and pause. The interior was sheltered from view by smoked glass and opera curtains. It was not until I was pushed inside that I saw Lilah blindfolded and gagged with her arms fastened behind her on a Moroccan leather rear jump-seat.

The flower child-thug climbed over me and seated herself behind the driver's seat with the gun in her hand. A smoked glass partition separated the front from the rear seat, and I was only able to glimpse a dark-haired fellow in what looked like a very well-tailored blazer and ascot—not a Beverly Hills, but a Peal & Co. of London look. The car glided away from the curb, and with a smooth whine the partition slid down.

Barely turning his elegant razor-trimmed head, the man in the driver's seat began to speak.

"Welcome. My name is Victor. You may not be

familiar with me, but permit me the liberty of confessing my admiration for your journalism, Mr. Davenport. Under less infelicitous circumstances we could have had some provocative conversations about journalism and fiction and the deliberate confusion of the two realms you seem to delight in." He spoke with the elaborate locutions of someone trying to sound like William F. Buckley—and failing to bring it off.

"But for now," he continued, "I am under contract, after a fashion, to deliver you up to Colonel Atila, who particularly enjoys experimenting with a new advance in technologically induced truth-telling developed by the secret police of his country. A device known as the Feedback Lie Detector, a machine that combines the lie-detecting capability of voice and autonomic nervous system parameters with an electroshock capability. Properly calibrated, the machine automatically registers a response's lack of truthfulness and immediately delivers a controllable, automatic surgical strike of unbearable pain. Skinnerians like to call it 'negative reinforcement.'"

"You tell one little lie, you feel like a rusty scissor stabbed through your brain," said the flower child-thug.

"You must excuse Laurel's colorful street language, but I was only recently and with great difficulty able to rescue her from life as a child porn star."

"Victor rescued me from exploitation and degradation," Laurel said with great conviction and reverence. "It was terrible, just terrible. I knew I had talent and all the people around me knew I had talent, but my manager had no confidence in me and he had me locked into a contract where he got all the residuals. Now that Victor manages me, I haven't had to give up my career just because of age, the way it happened to some people I know. Not many child porn stars can make the crossover to adult work. And *none* of them get to do the kind of things like I did today. How did you say it, Victor? You always have the right words."

"Participating in the creation of literary history, my dear."

Victor glanced back at me and gave a gleaming, ingratiating grin.

"I suppose Lilah has told you about my, shall we call them, 'literary services' or 'introductions,' so there's no harm in revealing the essence of Laurel's assignment last night, although as for the name . . . Let's just say he was a very, very major American novelist. And when I saw him outside Elaine's last week he had a difficult literary problem. He was attempting a very serious exploration of the meaning of the Sixties, re-creating in a novel what we academic types refer to as the myth of *The American Adam*, after the book by that name. His problem was to recapture the deliquescent innocence, the blood-surging vitality and the compliant sensuality of that re-created Eve, the flower child. He felt the need to guide his grand design with the evidences of his senses, as he put it. And so, although Laurel is not technically a flower child in the strictest sense of the phrase, when I introduced Laurel to him . . ."

"He just about drooled all over the seat," Laurel interjected. "But it got better after I got him to take a couple of 'ludes."

"He was extremely enthusiastic about how much he learned from her, and I feel confident that Laurel's labor of love tonight will, transmuted in the forge of novelistic genius, become a memorable scene in the postmodernist canon."

"Victor, do you think he'll put all the things he made me say, like, during, in an actual novel?"

"You can never tell with artists, dear."

"Victor," I said. "Could I ask a question at this point?"

"Shoot," said Victor.

"Which one?" said Laurel.

"Not now, Laurel. I didn't mean it that way. Please go ahead," Victor said to me.

"My first question is can you maybe drop me off at my place on your way uptown? This has been fascinating and all, but I've got some calls to make. What say we get together for lunch some time, Victor? I'm leaving for Samoa in a couple of days, but what we could do is pencil something in for when I get back."

Victor chuckled indulgently. "I think you have a greater appreciation of the gravity of the situation than you let on. Certainly if you don't now, you will when the Colonel straps you into his special lie detector machine."

"Well, I'm looking forward to that, but in the meanwhile, could you tell me why Lilah has to be blindfolded and gagged and I'm not?"

"Now there's a good reporter's question. As a matter of fact we're going to remedy that momentarily by putting a blindfold on you. You see, the place we're going to isn't supposed to exist any more. It got conveniently lost during the final days of the Nixon presidency, and those of us who know about it don't want it to be found again. It's become very useful. It's a very special place. Perhaps in your Watergate meanderings you may have come across a mention of it. It's the lost trysting place of the Golden Greek."

I tried to play dumb. "The Golden Greek. You don't mean that scheme the Plumbers had to blackmail the Chappaquiddick girls."

"Very good," said Victor, "I compliment your memory retention in the face of all the drugs you seem to ravage your body with. It's an obscure Watergate footnote many have forgotten."

"Weren't they going to set up some Adonis type in a plush apartment with hidden cameras, then let him loose to snare one of the women who were on Chappaquiddick with Teddy Kennedy that night? They were supposed to film the Golden Greek fucking this woman and try to blackmail her into telling the real story of Chappaquiddick?"

"Indeed," Victor said, "there is public testimony such plans were discussed."

"But nothing ever came of it, right? The Greek turned out to be a flop in the seduction game."

"That is the consensus of the public testimony," Victor said.

"I mean, wasn't it in John Dean's book that he describes being given the key to the Greek's place by Caulfield or Ulasiewicz to use for a New York date, and he walks in with this woman he's trying to impress and finds this place covered with pink shag rugs and gilt mirrors, all red and black leather like some fancy Chicago whorehouse."

Victor sighed and swung the car over to an exit off the FDR Drive, reflectively muttering, "There was a problem with the décor at first."

"You're telling me *you* worked on the Golden Greek scheme?"

"Please. The so-called Golden Greek did not stay with the project long, nor did Caulfield or Ulasiewicz, thank God. Some new people took charge. Some people who meant business and had the budget to follow through. There was a substantial redecorating job to be done—I worked with the decorator myself— and substantial retargeting too. Let's just say I made some of my services available."

Victor pulled the Bentley over to the curb on a quiet side street near East End Avenue. "Laurel, please put the blindfold on the gentleman in the back. I hope

you'll realize that this is an act of concern for your
well-being. If the Colonel did not explicitly instruct me
to bring you to him blindfolded, he might under some
circumstances feel you could not be allowed back alive
with the knowledge of his location."

Laurel fastened the blindfold, which reeked with
strawberry incense, around my head.

"And if things go well," Victor added, "and you
don't try to lie to the Colonel's vengeful lie-detecting
device, we may take the blindfolds off and allow you to
see some of the videotapes made in the apartment.
There are some you might particularly enjoy, some
certain segments reveal Lilah at her most delightfully
spontaneous and uninhibited."

"Uh, Victor, when you said 'retargeting' of the
Golden Greek mission, just what did that mean?"

"Do you think that they were about to dismantle
all that expensive apparatus, the whole setup, just
because Teddy dropped out of the race? Uh-uh. They
just reverted to what had always been the target all
along—the Eastern media establishment. Think of it.
If you're Nixon and you're talking to the head of the
documentary division of one of the networks about
some conflict-of-interest scandal he's onto, wouldn't
you feel more confident if you had a videotape of the
network guy sitting around naked, blitzed on acid he's
been slipped and gibbering like a chimp? Remember,
they tried to put acid on Jack Anderson's steering
wheel. It was a pet fantasy of the Plumbers. And if

you're dealing with the managing editor of a news magazine who's asking about your tax returns, wouldn't you like the security of having this guardian of public morality on tape wallowing in peanut butter and jelly with two child porn stars?"

"Once an old guy asked me to use peanut butter on him," Laurel said. "The thing was I got Skippy Super Chunky style by mistake and . . ."

"Wait a minute, Victor," I said. "Are you telling me that they actually went ahead with this?"

"I've seen the videotapes," he said. "For a time I had custody of them. They could put a lot of powerful people out of commission in one way or another. By the time the Watergate hearings began, these things were just too hot, too seamy to add to the mess.

"Remember when E. Howard Hunt asked for a cool million to keep quiet about certain 'seamy things' he knew the White House was involved in?" Victor went on. "You think he was just talking about the Ellsberg break-in? This operation made that one look like an ACLU picnic. Very, very seamy. I don't even feel good about my role in it although all I did was make some introductions."

"Did they actually make use of these to blackmail—?"

"That's something I don't know, although from what I saw on the tapes I can make educated guesses. It was a very powerful, very dirty weapon, so dirty that once the heat started building on Watergate, the whole thing would have blown up in their faces if they made a move to use it. Eventually, when the search warrants and the indictments began to come down, I was given custody of them, for safekeeping, with the right to burn them if I felt it appropriate."

"You have them?"

"Had them. One night at Elaine's I made the terrible mistake of hinting to Walter Foster that I could arrange an unusual screening for him," Victor sighed. "I have a fatal weakness for attempting to ingratiate myself with Elaine's set, and Foster was pumping me as usual on the subject of women I knew who had slept with the Kennedys. He was obsessed with the subject; he wanted to know everything down to the most clinical detail about them. And he wanted me to introduce him to them. And I did. I think he felt something, something he lacked that the Kennedys had, might rub off on him from their women. I think he fancied himself the JFK of the media. Anyway, that night when I hinted that one of these women might be viewed in all her splendor dallying with a network anchorman, Foster threatened to bar me from his table in Elaine's unless I arranged a private screening for him. What could I do?"

"It must have been a difficult moral dilemma," I said.

"It's easy for you to laugh," Victor sighed. "You probably think I'm nothing more than a pimp with pretensions. Someday I'd like to outline to you the much-neglected dignity of the pimp's role in literary tradition. Start with the figure of Pandarus in Chaucer's *Troilus and Cryseyde,* who unlike the lewd and degraded pander in Shakespeare's *Troilus and Cressida* can be seen as a godlike creative presence, drawing the two lovers out of the encapsuled solipsism of the conventions of courtly love and into the communion of a common bed.

"Indeed, the pimp should be looked upon as a muse figure, a go-between who brings together the realm of experience and the realm of imaginative inspiration. I wrote a thesis on the subject at Princeton—that's what I was doing until I got into supplying women to the media covering the Kennedy campaign. But later, after I had established myself as a go-between with a more literary crowd, I realized I was doing something more than any English scholar could ever do—I wasn't merely *explicating* literature, I was *expediting* it."

Victor's obvious pride in his literary sophistication gave me an idea. It was a long shot, but I remembered the advice various experts had recently been giving corporate executives on how to handle a political kidnapping: try to establish some kind of common human relationship with your captors—it made it more difficult for them to dispose of you casually. I could hardly have expected the explosive results of the gambit I was about to play.

"Listen, Victor," I began, "as one ex-English

major to another, I want to confide something to you
now, a secret I've been sitting on, not ready to publish
yet, but something that—well, you've got a gun and
Laurel there has a gun and I don't know where you're
taking us or whether I'll be coming back, but it's the
kind of thing I think a man of your taste and judgment
in literary matters will understand the sensational
importance of. Something I—"

"You don't want to die with, is that correct?"
Victor asked.

"What if I were to tell you," I said, lowering my
voice, "that I'd solved *'The Mystery of Edwin Drood'*?"

"Come now, don't tell me you're wasting your
time with that silly old chestnut. I thought only little
old ladies in tennis shoes who write letters to *The
Dickensian* concern themselves with that anymore. I
mean, without sounding too chauvinistically Princeton, is there anything more interesting to be said on
the question after Bunny Wilson's essay? I presume
you're familiar with that. Dickens' irreconcilable
ambivalence about the darker powers of his art and all
that."

"Ah, Victor. So you are familiar with the Drood
problem. I expect you to be skeptical, but at least I
know I'm dealing with a sophisticate in the literature."

"As I said, I'm only familiar with the so-called
problem through Bunny Wilson's essay. But really,
Davenport, there is no problem even on the most
primitive level. It's obvious what's-his-name, the

choirmaster, did away with Drood. I hope you're not wasting your time on some silly variant."

"Not quite a variant, Victor. But when I say I solved the Mystery of Edwin Drood, I'm not talking about the mystery of the murder of Drood. Yes, I know Jasper the choirmaster did it. I'm not talking about solving a literary puzzle, I'm talking about real murder—the murder of Charles Dickens himself."

"Dickens murdered? Come, come. He died a natural death, a stroke. Strenuous schedule of public readings killed him. In any event, why would anyone want to murder that most beloved author of all time?"

"To prevent him from publishing the final installments of *The Mystery of Edwin Drood.*"

"It wasn't that bad. I admit not my favorite, but—"

"I'm serious. Dickens was about to reveal something in the final installments. Something someone didn't want revealed. A ruinous scandal, a murder. Something in which Dickens himself might be implicated, subject to blackmail, perhaps only to shadow forth in fiction."

"Quite a lovely conceit, but what's the evidence? I hope it's not textual alone—the absurdities of the new criticism as practiced at your alma mater are tedious *in vacuo.*"

"In my apartment, Victor, I could show you citations from the available biographical data alone that make a strong circumstantial case. Just, for instance, consider Dickens' bizarre behavior in his final days. Consider the strange obsession with dramatic readings of the brutal murder of Nancy by Sikes from *Oliver Twist*. Consider his growing addiction to laudanum, when taken with the choirmaster's rehearsing the crime in an opium dream. Consider his obsessively secret adulteries which even your Bunny Wilson calls 'hushed up' by the biographers. Consider finally his obsessive repetition of a phrase from *Romeo and Juliet* toward the end. A phrase Friar Lawrence uses when he's describing the poison he's concocting: 'These violent delights have violent ends.' My theory is that the so-called apoplectic stroke was a fatal poisoning whose symptoms mimicked a violent but natural death. And that Dickens knew it was coming, knew someone would try to kill him, and tried to hint at it in the text. I could show you clues—"

"Enough already, for pity's sake," Victor said. "Let us accept *arguendo* our beloved author was murdered. Who did it? You must have a theory."

Despite his sarcastic tone, I had a feeling Victor was intrigued. I decided it would be unwise to tell him I was currently pursuing my research by smoking opium and trying to communicate with the visionary presence of the beloved author himself for the inside scoop on his own murder. It was the kind of thing that people who called the late Edmund Wilson "Bunny" might not cotton to.

"Well, I have a profile of the murderer. It's hard to get information on the darker side of Dickens' life, the 'hushed up' stuff, but until I find a smoking gun that points another way, I've got to assume that the key to the identity of the man who murdered Charles Dickens must lie in the character of the opium-smoking choirmaster, John Jasper."

"Well, again accepting *arguendo* that Dickens *was* murdered, the answer is quite obvious, isn't it?"

"What?" I never expected this. "Obvious? Who?"

"Well, let's put it this way. What intimate of Dickens was also a heavy, very heavy laudanum addict and opium smoker too? What literary figure was both protégé and rival of Dickens? A protégé whose first mystery novel surpassed Dickens' later work in popularity and may have actually inspired some plot elements in *Drood*?"

"Victor, you don't mean . . ."

"Of course I do: Wilkie Collins."

I had begun this as a diversion, but now I was floored by the idea that right here, blindfolded by a pimp and a thug in the back of a Bentley bound who-knows-where, the secret had been revealed. Wilkie Collins. The father of the English detective novel, himself a murderer. All those things Victor had said about him had been true. But he had been so close to Dickens. Dickens had given him his start. Had been an intimate companion and grateful protégé who had shared so much of his later years and—yes, now it began to make sense.

"My god, Victor, do you realize we may have solved the literary crime of the century?"

"I might take exception to your use of 'we' if I

thought the notion was more than a paranoid fantasy. But please, don't be tiresome and demand we pull over and let you out into a phone booth to call Scotland Yard or maybe ring up *Partisan Review* and tell them to stop the presses. We have an appointment to keep."

"My god, Victor. We *should* call a press conference."

"So long as you cooperate, there should be nothing to prevent you from appearing in public at some future time. For now, I would submit that we are about to enter a far more significant phenomenon in literary history. The place where the Golden Greek tapes were made. Ah, what you can learn about some of our modern writers' technique one can never get from dry biographical details. When I had the Golden Greek tapes, I felt I had the Rosetta Stone to mid-century American literary character."

"Victor, why have we gone around the block four times?" Laurel asked.

"That's very shrewd, Laurel, giving them the deliberately misleading impression that we've gone around the block four times so they won't be able to keep track of our actual route. Very shrewd."

I felt the car lurch sharply to the right and head down an incline. It felt like we were entering an underground garage.

"Wait a minute, Victor," I said. "You said you *had* the Golden Greek videotapes. What happened to them?"

"That's what the Colonel and I and a number of people would like to find out from you and Lilah. All I know is that not long after I showed Walter Foster those ex-Kennedy-girlfriend tapes, some experts broke into my place at the Dakota and took every single one of them. A week later Foster called up to ask for yet another showing of the Kennedy-girl tapes, and I accused him of engineering the break-in. He accused me of *faking* the break-in to keep the tapes out of his hands, and I accused him of accusing me of *that* to cover up the fact he ordered it.

"That's where matters stood when Foster got shot and the Colonel, who had been a client of mine from before his brief marriage to Lilah, expressed interest in using his new 'truth stimulator' toy—I think he prefers that over lie detector—to get some answers from Lilah on the subject of Foster's activities and the missing videotapes."

The stale and stifling air of the underground garage settled over me like a warm shroud after Laurel nudged me out of the air-conditioned Bentley. Still blindfolded, I was half-guided, half-shoved across the gritty concrete surface by Laurel and her gun.

"But what was Foster going to do with the tapes if he did manage to get them?"

"We all hope Lilah will be able to tell us the truth about that once she's strapped into the Colonel's machine, but I would suspect they might play a role in his ultimate revenge scheme."

"Revenge on who?"

"On whom," Victor the ex-English major corrected me. "On the entire literary media establishment. On Elaine's. It's odd. It wasn't so much that they took away his magazine from him, or his publishing company and his limo. Those he could get again. But when he lost his table at Elaine's something snapped. After that he no longer wanted a comeback. He wanted to tear down the whole fabric of literary society. I heard him once when I dropped down to the Caribbean to visit with the Colonel. We'd been drinking absinthe all night and I didn't know whether or not to believe his outburst."

We entered what seemed to be a freight elevator shaft. Victor's voice rose and echoed as he began an imitation of the late Walter Foster.

"'Victor,' he'd say to me, 'Victor, they got real pirate kings down here. They got *real* cutthroats. These smugglers and sharks, Old Joe Kennedy himself couldn't have made it in this league. I thought I was big-league. Christ, those people up at Elaine's, they thought I was fuckin' *Jaws 2* because I could chew out some pasty-faced pencil pushers. Can you fuckin' believe it? But let me tell you somethin' about those Elaine's assholes, Victor. Their day is coming, that's all I can say.'"

"Do you think he'd go as far as to use Nixon's last dirty trick just to get back his table at Elaine's?" I asked.

"He doesn't want his table back. He wants to bring the whole establishment crashing down on top of it."

"Hey, you guys," said Laurel. "Isn't it a little too late? This guy Foster is croaked already, right?"

"Yes, my dear," said Victor. "But that doesn't mean the plan can't go forward. If he's stored the tapes in a safe-deposit box with instructions for disposition upon death, a number of powerful people might want to find the key to that box. Wouldn't they, Lilah?" said Victor, chuckling.

Still gagged, Lilah did not attempt to respond.

Judging from the length of the ride, it was a high floor on which the elevator finally deposited us.

Down the hall I heard a faint electronic hum. A door opened. Pushed in by a gun butt, I stumbled blindly forward across a polished wooden floor. A strong and unfamiliar hand began guiding me down the length of several corridors and finally into a room with a rug that felt like the wide Sargasso Sea.

"Welcome," an unfamiliar neutral voice began. "My name is Dr. Manolo. The Colonel will be with you in a moment. In the meantime he has asked me to begin preparations. Please step up and seat yourselves in these chairs."

I wondered how Lilah was taking this. She had never told me much about her marriage to the Colonel. She ran away with him shortly after he was transferred from the Nicaraguan consulate back to Managua.

There he embroiled himself in the Machiavellian family politics of the fearful Somoza family. The Colonel—he got the rank from an early career in the secret police—claimed descent from a bastard black-sheep branch of the family and had been driven into exile, Lilah said, because of an intrigue he had concoct-ed with the powerful deputy of the state's secret police.

Once I'd seen a blurry AP wirephoto of the Col-onel in the company of Robert Letzgo, his most recent employer. The Colonel was a big man with a hatchet face and a hint of melancholy in his eyes.

"Welcome, my friends." It was the Colonel. He sounded as if he was standing right in front of me. "I apologize for the inhospitable gesture of removing your clothes and submitting you to the truth eliciter with such nonceremonious haste, but I feel a friend-ship founded upon truth, and thus trust, is the only true friendship." He spoke English flawlessly with only a trace of his Central American origins.

"Unfortunately, to attach the final set of elec-trodes, will require you to endure a regrettable indig-nity we will remedy when we are on more trusting terms. You see, with one's clothes off we have found one's parasympathetic nervous system is far more vulnerable and sensitive to the stress of deception. Don't you feel that's instinctively true, Lilah, my dear? You needn't answer. Of course you can't until I remove that gag, but I think we'll wait until we've tied you up to the machine. Dr. Manolo, do you think you can secure the electrodes to their bodies?"

I felt cool swabs of alcohol wipe my temples, my jaw—and, after the regrettable indignity the Colonel referred to—my genitals. Sticky adhesive-covered wires were affixed to those areas.

"Perhaps afterward, Colonel," said Victor, "you can tell our friend from the media about your idea for a television show featuring your machine. The Colonel wants to do a *real* Truth or Consequences, with public figures wired up this way. Am I not right, Colonel?"

"It's true. I believe your Mr. Frank Silverman would be sympatico with the kind of honesty I can bring to TV programming. I hope our friend from the media will be candid enough with us so that he's in condition to chat about my idea, Victor. Perhaps he can introduce me to Mr. Silverman. There's no sense in squirming in your chair, Lilah," I heard the Colonel say. "As long as you tell me the truth it will be as if we were having a simple husband and wife talk. It is good to see you once again in the flesh, shall I say, my dear.

"Although I must say your flesh has been featured on some provocative videotapes, as I understand it—we hope you can help us find them all. You've learned some amusing diversions since our ill-starred marriage. Don't think I'm being an old-fashioned, vengeful husband. Quite the contrary, I hope you will not subject yourself to unnecessarily debilitating pain in resisting the truth-eliciting power of my machine. Dr. Manolo, will you ready the sensors?" I began to hear a low electronic hum coming from the center of the room.

"I understand Victor has briefed both of you on the ability of this machine to combine lie detecting with a lie-punishing capacity that works directly upon the particularly sensitive eye, teeth, and genital pain centers within the brain. Should you choose to remain silent, the operator has the discretion to unleash the pain-stimulation capability alone to stimulate you to talk.

"Clever machine, is it not? The secret police of my country are very good. Only too narrow-minded, as alas all technicians seem to be. They are afraid to publicize this marvelous invention because they fear that it will arouse outcries from the human-rights zealots, who see it as an instrument of 'clean' torture that leaves no telltale marks for their pesty inspection committees to tattle about. But I say, let's shout it from the rooftops—here is a device that will usher in an age of total truth-telling. Lies and secrets will disappear from the earth because they can be exposed so efficiently."

"Sounds like the dawning of the Age of Aquarius we've all been waiting for," I suggested.

"Indeed, that is not so far-fetched," the Colonel went on. "I regret the necessity for the use of pain as a truth eliciter at this stage of the machine's development—we've had some promising results in experiments with electrically stimulating the guilt centers of the cortex, so that someone who has told a lie will suffer an immediate and unbearable attack of remorse and will weepingly confess the truth. But until then there is only pain. Let's begin with you, Lilah. Remember, the truth will set you free. Dr. Manolo, will you remove the gag? Now, Lilah," the Colonel said, pronouncing his words slowly and deliberately. "Did you kill Walter Foster?"

I held my breath in the silence that followed. Then I heard Lilah start to say, "Of course not." Then I heard her start to scream.

In the painful silence that followed Lilah's screams the Colonel began to chuckle quietly. I heard the pervasive electronic hum step up in pitch. I heard the Colonel's next question: "Tell me, Lilah, exactly why *did* Walter Foster ask you to meet him at Elaine's last night?"

Then I heard the sound of wood splintering and cracking. No trouble recognizing the sound: someone was kicking in the door to the apartment suite.

THE CONSOMMÉ
IS SERVED

his was the third time in the six hours since
Lilah had come bursting in on my opium dream
at 4:00 A.M. that I'd been in a room in which
the door had been kicked open. I would have been more
surprised to hear a simple knock.

What did startle me was the voices of these intrud-
ers. Two very familiar voices: I heard them just a few
hours ago in the slab room of the morgue. That Irish

rasp was Inspector "Hickory Dick" Dockery, the head
of the NYPD's unofficial "celebrity homicide squad."
That manic jabber was Saperstein, the cabala-crazed
ex-neurosurgeon turned morgue wagon man who had
dragged Walter Foster's dead body out from under his
table at Elaine's earlier this morning.

Dockery was barking orders at the Colonel, the
Colonel's doctor, Victor, and his flower-child thug.
Evidently Dockery had a gun, because the orders were
being obeyed. Finally he turned his attention to Lilah
and me, still naked and blindfolded and strapped to
the Colonel's "electroshock lie-detector" chairs.

"Get the blindfolds off those two, Saperstein. And
the clothes on. Or maybe their goddamn clothes on
first and then take the blindfolds off. Mother of God.
I do my best to preserve some decency in the conduct
of my duties, but it's a losing battle, and a thankless
one."

"Thank you, Inspector, sir," said Lilah, exagger-
ating her Texas drawl a bit. "As a Southern woman I
always appreciate a man who attempts to uphold some
standards in this world."

"In fact, Inspector, maybe *you* should put on a
blindfold until we get dressed," I suggested. This
attempt at levity struck the Inspector as ill-timed.

"Listen, sonny," he snarled. "You know the max
for possession with intent to sell on an opium rap; my
men came up with enough in a twenty-minute search
of your place to have you doing twenty years if you

look at me crosswise, and even if you don't, I might book you into a section of the Tombs the ACLU ain't heard of and get you raped and stomped before anyone knows you're missing. So don't go breakin' my balls with wise-ass shit. Understand?"

I nodded weakly.

"Okay," Dockery resumed. "Saperstein here and I have business to take care of, and we know you folks can help us because between the six of you, we're going to find out precisely who killed Walter Foster."

"Inspector, sir," the Colonel said, "please be assured that as a former consular official of the Nicaraguan government, I too have an interest in the orderly process of judgment and would offer you the use of these sophisticated lie-detection devices to aid in your search. We all want the truth to come out."

"Listen, General Wetback, don't blow smoke up my pipes. I happen to know your consulate would love to turn you over to your relatives for an orderly process of torture and execution, so don't tempt me. Because as I'm about to explain, you may all decide you're better off if the truth does *not* come out. Let me explain to you ladies and gentlemen some new things Saperstein and I have learned about the murder of Walter Foster, and why all of you are going to cooperate with me."

Dockery took off his sweat-stained jacket and began pacing the rug. "I feel dirty," he began. "I found out a lot more about the literary life in the last few hours than I ever wanted to know. I learned enough about the media to elect Agnew in '84. All night I've been grilling these hotshots from Elaine's, and I've never seen such a guilty-looking lot. At first none of them can explain just what they happen to be doing in Manhattan on this particular Sunday night in August. I hear in that racket they break your knuckles if they catch you leaving the Hamptons on a weekend. They came to town on 'business,' they say.

"Bullshit, I say. Perjury is one to five, I explain to them. Then one by one they spill it." The Inspector's voice rose to a mock falsetto. "'Well yes, Inspector, it's *so* embarrassing that . . . well, I *did* receive this picture in the mail.' Black and white glossy. Definitely not family hour material if you know what I mean. Divorce court material. Contract cancellation type material. Moral-leper type material.

"It's amazing some of the things people will do. Each of them gets an 8 x 10 reminder in the mail last week with a note. Three words: *Elaine's. Closing Time.* And a date: *Sunday, August 20.* Last night. Now I question them about these pictures. I don't ask them about the underage girls; I don't ask them about the German shepherds and the drugs in the pictures with them. I just ask, 'Where? Where were you when you were doing these filthy disgusting things?' And it turns out it was right here. In this room. It took me five fucking hours to piece together an address from these media jerkoffs. You people didn't have to work as hard as I did. You knew the address, and you came right here after Walter Foster's murder. I'd say it looks bad for all of you, especially when your collateral illegal activities become the subject of close scrutiny. As I look around the room I see kidnapping raps, I see heavyweight smuggling raps, I see opium possession, I see pimping and soliciting, blackmail, conspiracy . . . you name it—not to mention murder.''

"Inspector.'' It was the Colonel. The Inspector sighed. "Inspector, perhaps some of these people could be persuaded to be philosophical about this little business of the pictures in the mail. Cite to them the example of one of my country's most popular leaders. He found himself approached by men who identified themselves as KGB. They showed him movies of a particularly strenuous party—well, let's be frank and call it a frenzied orgy—in which he'd had the pleasure to participate. The puritanical KGB bureaucrats were certain it was powerful blackmail material. Instead, our leader beamed and told them, 'I like this film. My people will be very proud of me.' Perhaps a more cosmopolitan attitude on the part of . . .''

"Enough. God, it kills me that I might have to let you off. There's nothing I'd like more than to see all you cosmopolitan scum festering in a hole. But I got more important things to think of. Doctor Saperstein here has come up with something that changes the rules of this case entirely. Saperstein, my boy, are you set to operate?''

I turned around to see Saperstein, all six-foot-six

of him in his white morgue wagon jacket stained with who knows what, fussing intently with a portable cassette recorder.

It was the first time since my blindfold had been removed that I had a chance to take a good look at what once had been the bedroom of the videotaped love-nest the President's Plumbers had prepared for the Golden Greek and his talented successors. I say what *once* had been the bedroom because there was no bed there. There wasn't much of anything in the high-ceilinged, white-walled chamber. It looked as if there had been a furniture sale—everything hastily carted away to raise cash for last-minute hush-money payments as the coverup collapsed. All gone except the pink shag rug, the track spotlights, and the mirrors. Across the field of pink shag, Saperstein knelt in a corner of the room covered with wall and ceiling mirrors, a corner where once the bed had been, and where, once upon a mattress, the Golden Greek and friends had cavorted for the hidden cameras behind the one-way mirrors.

"I want you all to listen very closely to the tape Saperstein is going to play for you," Dockery said. "At firs. Saperstein didn't want to play it even for me. At first he didn't want me to know he had it. It's just a little cassette. It fell out of Walter Foster's suit jacket pocket when Saperstein was wrapping up the stiff at Elaine's, Saperstein says. He pocketed it by mistake, he says, and in the excitement of seeing all those big literary types all around he just forgot to hand it over, he says. Then I'm down in the slab room and I hear voices. And what do you know—it's Saperstein in the baby locker crouching over a cassette machine. He tried to tell me it was just a tape of some Lubavitcher Hasidic holy man chanting he liked to play for inspiration. But I decided to listen to it anyway. That wasn't quite the case, was it, Saperstein?"

Saperstein remained silent. "But I listened," Dockery continued. "And now we're all gonna listen so you'll understand why you're going to cooperate with us. Pay attention to this tape. It's only eighteen-and-a-half minutes long."

Saperstein depressed the play button. At first there was just static. Then the recognizable sounds of furniture shifting, and the clink of silverware against china, emerged from the static. And then that unmistakable voice—suddenly it was perfectly clear who was talking.

"Uh, Steward, I will have some of that consommé."

Pause.

"Oh, hello, Bob. Come in. It's been, uh, a busy weekend for us all. I never do get time to relax at Key Biscayne. Uh, Ehrlichman was in here a little while ago and, uh, it looks like there may be some problem areas and—yes, come in steward, set it down here and please close the door behind you on the way out. Now, Bob . . ."

"Hold it," I said. "Dockery, you're not trying to

tell me this is a White House tape. I mean sure, it *sounds* like him, but come on."

"Not *a* White House tape," Dockery replied. "*The* White House tape. The eighteen-and-a-half-minute-gap tape. Not the original reel-to-reel Secret Service tape, but a direct, first-generation transcription of what's on that tape. More people have wanted to hear what's on this than on any single piece of tape in history. Now, do you want to listen or do you want to jabber questions?"

"But it was erased. Five times. How could . . ."

"The White House original was erased. But theirs wasn't the only bug in the Oval Office. Shut up and listen. I'll explain later. Well, maybe so you can appreciate the whole thing, I should set the scene for what you're going to hear for the next eighteen minutes, and there won't be so many dumb questions."

Dockery resumed pacing the expanse of pink shag.

"It's Tuesday morning, June 20, 1972, three days after the five burglars were arrested inside the Watergate. The *Washington Post* and the FBI are already on the trail of Hunt and Liddy and the White House connection. If they get them and get them to talk, the whole White House including the Trick himself could break out into assholes and shit itself to death, if you know what I mean. They're trying to patch together a coverup, but it looks shaky. They need something to keep the media quiet. Haldeman comes in the Oval Office for a strategy session that morning, and as soon as the steward leaves, the prez begins to lay out his counterattack plan. It's at that very point that someone in the White House repeatedly erased the tape and left us with an eighteen-minute buzz.

"What were they really talking about?" Dockery continued. "The special prosecutor got hold of the handwritten notes Haldeman supposedly took during that eighteen minutes. You read them and they sound pretty abstract—'What is our counterattack? P.R. offensive to top this, hit the opposition with their activities. We should be on the attack for diversion.' That's all he wrote. Not too many details, doesn't seem to fill up eighteen minutes, does it? Want to hear what they were really saying? Go, Saperstein."

The morgue man depressed the play button again, and once again that unmistakable voice.

"And, uh, Bob, as we talk about our counterattack, we have to keep in mind it's the presidency we're defending. Because this Watergate is a scab now, but the media will pick on it till it bleeds, and when they scent blood, they'll all come and wallow in it. And it's, uh, no skin off my ass, but it's off the ass of the presidency. Which is why I say no more Mr. Nice Guy for me. When I say P.R. offensive on their activities, I don't mean just public relations. I mean private relations too. Have you ever seen the, uh, so-called Golden Greek tapes?"

"No. But I've heard rumors about the project. The naked network executives. Uh, isn't that seamy stuff, Mr. President?"

"The time has come for a bold move. Full steam ahead. Like I did with China, which was my idea and not Henry's, if you recall. We are entering a fight to the death with the media over who will govern this country, and I have a constitutional obligation to defend the presidency with all the means at my disposal. And I say it's time to expose the depravity of these so-called guardians of public morality. Or, heh, heh, let them expose themselves. Hold them up to pubic scrutiny before a shocked nation."

"You mean public, sir?"

"Public scrutiny. Let it all hang out, give the public the bare facts, the unmodified, unlimited hang-out route, let them . . ."

"But sir, what about the backlash?"

"Yes, they do that too. And not only on the back. But one thing is for sure, the presidency will not be their whipping boy. Bob, I'm going to show you something the Plumbers have put together for me."

"It looks like some kind of big television set, sir."

"No, Bob. I don't mean the set. I mean this cassette I'm going to show on it. The machine is called a Betamax. Brand-new thing. Gift of the Japanese ambassador. Wonderful people, the Japanese. Their ancient culture and all. Although I don't understand this eating of raw fish. But all you do is put a videocassette on and switch it like so and . . ."

Military music drowned out the conversation for a moment.

"Mr. President, we've already watched *Patton* several times this week down in the screening room. Don't you think that . . ."

"Sorry, Bob, wrong cassette. Here. This is the one. This cassette is a short compilation of the most abandoned, drugged, and decadent scenes from the so-called Golden Greek project. These were made after the Golden Greek himself was dismissed, and we approved a retargeting to the media cabal. We haven't synched-in the sound track, but you'll recognize a lot of these people instantly."

Silence in the Oval Office as the two most powerful men in the free world riveted themselves to the scenes on the Betamax screen. Occasionally there would be a comment in a hushed, strained voice.

"Ooh, look at that. And the media have the nerve to accuse us of 'illegal entry.' She can't be more than 14."

"Hey, now, that's a strange scene. That woman looks like she's got her tit caught in a wringer or something."

"It must be one of those strange S&M scenes that crowd goes for."

More silence.

"Get a load of the big enchilada on that guy."

"So that's why they call him an anchorman."

"Yeah, but it looks like it's turning out to be inoperative, huh? Ziegler will like that."

"Yeah. A pitiful, helpless giant."

Pause. Shifting chairs. Coughs.

"Uh, Bob, is, uh, what she's doing there—is that, uh, what they call 'Deep Six'?"

"No, actually, I think the phrase is 'Deep Throat'."

"Deep Throat, huh, I'll have to remember that. What an exciting prospect."

"Well, you could say that guy is gonna be Deep Six with his network when they see him in this film."

"Gee. Will you look at that, though. Some syndicated columnists do everything together."

"Yes. But catch this. I never would have believed a guy like that . . . such a family man."

"You never can tell, just because they have a wife and kids. Goddamn media, they talk about our bugging when they're buggering each other everyday."

"That one looks like a third-rate buggery to me."

"Well, this is the tail end of the tape, if you know what I mean. Steward, I will have some of that consommé. By the way, Bob, did you know, I learned something about buggery from one of these goddamn Harvard assholes Henry is always bringing around. It is kind of funny. We were talking about Bulgaria and Yugoslavia, and he remarked that the word *bugger* is derived from Bulgaria, because of some tribe of homo Christian heretics or something who became famous in Bulgaria."

"Makes you wonder what the real meaning of Yugoslavia is, heh, heh."

"It could be quite Tito-lating."

"Well, I'm not Balkan at the idea."

There followed a lot of snickering and gleeful obscenities that made me wonder if "some of that consommé" the President was repeatedly consuming might be a code phrase—since Nixon knew he was always on tape and you never heard him ordering a drink—for a more volatile substance fueling this giddiness. Then I heard a click as the cassette in Saperstein's machine came to a halt.

Nobody said a word for a while. My mouth was dry with excitement. I could have used "some of that consommé" myself. Having covered the great coverup trial back in '75, having listened on press section earphones to the White House tapes played for the jury, I had no doubt it was the same Oval Office voices I was hearing. Of course I should add that I'd ingested a bit of "Mr. Natural" blotter acid before entering the trial room that day, and sometime later I heard Mr. Natural's voice too, although I don't think it was on the same tape. But still, this tape I'd just heard *had* to be real: who would fake a ridiculous pun like "Tito-lating" if he wanted anyone to believe it. It's one of those awful things that people only say in real life.

"But how could it be real?" I blurted out to Dockery. "That tape was erased over and over again. The Trick got calluses doing it."

"Sure, they erased their tape. But not long after that they learned about the second taping system."

"The what?"

"You heard me. There've been articles hinting at it; it's an open secret in the intelligence community that a certain agency was aware of the Trick's private bugs from the word go. They had lines into the Plumbers, lines into the White House itself. It was no problem to tap the incoming voice pickups."

"You're saying the CIA was taping Nixon's tapes all along?"

"Everybody knows Nixon and the CIA were playing a heavy game of mutual blackmail behind the scenes during Watergate. Read Ehrlichman's novel. The Trick had a load of shit he could dump—CIA assassinations, drug dealing, the lot. But the agency had some heavy shit on him. They knew about the Plumbers, the bugs—and they had the tapes of the White House tapes. Everybody used to wonder why Nixon didn't go the 'bonfire option'—burn his tapes and say fuck off. Or resign and take the goddamn tapes home to San Clemente with him instead of letting all his enemies strangle him with them. I'll tell you why; because he knew, the agency let him know, *there was a second set of tapes* around with all those incriminating conversations on them. They were haunting him constantly—he never knew when, or if, they'd slip out. Deliberately, they never let him know. It was psychological warfare. They tormented the guy. And it cut the heart out of the counterattack you heard him planning. That kind of massive sexual blackmail against the media had to be done so the White House had absolute deniability. But no matter how many times he erased his own tape of him planning that shit, he knew the CIA could rub his nose in it. He was paralyzed, he just couldn't use the Golden Greek tapes."

"Pardon me, Inspector." It was the Colonel. "This is certainly a most enlightening view of how democracy works in your country, but what does all this have to do with the murder of Walter Foster?"

"Figure it out. Foster gets hold of the eighteen-minute gap, a copy of it anyway. How he gets it I don't exactly know yet, but the timing gives you a hint. The White House and the CIA were covering up for each other until The Trick resigned. As soon as he's out, all the heavy CIA shit starts to come out—the assassinations, the drugs. There's a purge inside the CIA, and the guys who were deep into that shit in the agency are on the outside now. Foster had the contacts. He'd done work for those guys. Maybe one of them gets to talking to Walter Foster down in the Caribbean. Foster gets the gap tape. He listens to The Trick going wild over the Golden Greek tapes. He knows Victor here has supplied most of the women and teenyboppers for the entertainment and has custody of the tapes. Victor sells them to Foster, or maybe Victor gets himself a cut out of the blackmail take which—"

"Inspector, please, I must object," said Victor primly. "I did not sell those tapes. They were entrusted to me by some people. Recently my apartment in the Dakota was broken into. It was a professional job. They took nothing but the tapes. Perhaps the professionals were working for Walter Foster; perhaps he was working for them. But I had no dealings with Walter Foster over tapes until he called me up to accuse *me* of staging the burglary, to throw suspicion on *him*, if you can imagine that."

"I could imagine that," said Dockery. "But I have a very vivid imagination. Most prosecutors I know—they don't have that kind of vivid imagination. They have these petty, one-track minds. They'll be thinking extortion, extortion, extortion all the time you're telling them your story. Which is why you and the rest of these storytellers are going to cooperate with me when I finish my story, even if I have to use a little extortion to get me that cooperation. Where was I? Okay. Foster has the eighteen-minute gap. Somehow he tracks down the Golden Greek videotapes. Gets them from Victor. He's got some grand scheme to use them to get his table back at Elaine's or get back at the people at the other tables. Mother of God, who would believe anyone would go to all that trouble over a crummy table? But I've just come from talking with that Elaine's crowd, and for these people it's a goddamned *matter of life or death.*

"So what does it add up to? Somebody inside Elaine's found out what Foster was up to. Maybe somebody who received one of those 8 x 10 pictures in the mail; maybe a friend of one of those guys who writes about the Mafia asked for an introduction to someone; maybe there was a contract taken out on him by the literary crowd. On the other hand, maybe it was some friends of The Trick himself, like your employer, Colonel—Mr. Letzgo down in the Caribbean. Maybe he found out Foster had the gap tape and decided Foster had to be erased to keep the gap silent. I don't know yet exactly which party ordered the hit, but maybe they needed to set up a beautiful young woman to lure him to the site of the hit. Or maybe the beautiful young lady had reasons of her own for wanting Walter Foster dead. We know the gun was hers, and her prints are on the gun. I dusted it myself. She has a lot to lose in the way of years in jail if she doesn't play along with Saperstein and me the way I'm sure the rest of you will."

Lilah looked flushed and worn. "Inspector, I know how pleased you must be with yourself for having cracked the case," she said, still able to summon her best Southern-belle sarcasm. "But I know how absolutely relentless you New York detectives are in your desire to see justice done; so I would be doing *you* an injustice if I didn't explain to you why you've got the whole damn thing ass-backward.

"You say someone, probably me, killed Walter Foster to prevent him from making some tapes public. Did you ever consider the possibility that he was killed *in order* to make the tapes public?"

"You're not trying to sell me some story about the CIA snuffing him to surface the gap, are you?"

"No. I'm saying he killed himself in order to sink the whole Elaine's establishment with the waves his death would make," Lilah declared. "Because he figured a spectacular murder investigation would surface not only that tape in his pocket, but a whole ton of tapes—videotapes made right here, which he'd hidden away somewhere. He told me something about a safe-deposit-box key that I would find in case anything had happened to him. I haven't found it, but I'm sure it would lead to those tapes, which was just what he—"

"Hold it there, young lady," Dockery interjected. "Saperstein, did you find any sort of safe-deposit or any other key on Foster's person?"

"No, Inspector," the morgue man replied, "and as you know, I looked very thoroughly." I looked at Saperstein very thoroughly. It seemed to me that he was trying to maintain a poker face, which meant he did not have a very convincing poker face.

"All right, young lady, perhaps before you try to explain how he committed suicide when your prints are on the gun, you can warm up with an easy one. Why were you there with him last night, and what exactly *was* your relationship to the late Mr. Foster?"

"It was almost two years ago that I first met him," Lilah began. "Victor introduced us, or should I say, Victor put him on to me. God, was he ever on to me.

He seaplaned out to my place in the Keys after Victor had primed him with Joe Kennedy stories: how my little island house was once the headquarters of old Joe's Caribbean bootlegging empire—and I'm sure you didn't leave out the rumors about old Joe and my mother and the question of whose child I am, did you, Victor?

"Kennedy blood," she continued. "Some people are mesmerized by the hint of Kennedy blood. I don't know who he wanted more—me or what he saw of old Joe in me. He didn't get either. It's funny, the Kennedy thing. I think for Walter Foster, Elaine's was once his Camelot. And they took away his little roundtable."

Lilah stood up. "That was the last time I saw him until last night. Oh, he called me, he wrote me, he sent emissaries. Then last week he sent me a calling card I couldn't ignore. It was an 8 x 10 black-and-white picture that looked as if it might have been snapped off a TV screen. If you must know, the picture revealed me and a certain celebrated consumer advocate, on a bed, ah, consumer-testing, you might say, the effectiveness of certain exotic devices. I'm not ashamed of that evening, but I was upset about the damage it might do to his cause if the picture fell into the wrong hands. Well, who should happen to call the day after but Walter Foster. He didn't admit to sending the photo, of course. Instead he told me some wild tale about people threatening his life, breaking into his place, trying to blackmail *him*. He told me he had to have a gun to protect himself, and said if I'd bring it with me to Elaine's we could discuss common measures against our common problem. I was dead certain he was the 'problem,' but I had to meet him to find out what his game was."

"Why would he come to you for a gun?" Dockery asked.

"I may look like a frail, delicate flower of Southern womanhood to you, Inspector, but my daddy grew up in Dalhart, Texas, and he taught me more about guns by the time I was ten than half the men on your force know now. Foster had seen my gun collection down at the Key, of course." Lilah paused. "But I don't think it was just my gun he wanted to use that night. He wanted my body too."

"You mean he . . ."

"No. Not that way. Not last night. Last night he wanted my body for his obituary. What I mean is, I think he was planning the suicide to look like murder, but he didn't want the obit to read 'shot while dining alone.' With me along he gets 'shot while dining with a lovely young woman.'"

"Are you sure it shouldn't be 'shot *by* a lovely young woman'?" Dockery asked Lilah. "All you've just said makes it sound even more likely you did it. Motive: blackmail. Case closed. If he wanted to release those Golden Greek tapes so badly, why'd he have to kill himself to do it? Why not just release 'em and stick around to watch the shit hit the fan?"

"That's what I'm getting to, Inspector. He explained the entire thing—why it had to be suicide. I tried to talk him out of it, but he had it all planned from the very moment we sat down at the table. First thing, he wanted to make sure the gun I'd brought him was loaded. I pushed my pocketbook under the table to him. Then in so many words he admitted he was responsible for that picture I got in the mail. He said it came from the tapes and that for playing along with him he was having the originals delivered to my apartment downtown, along with a safe-deposit-box key. He told me to destroy the tapes and mail the key to the homicide squad if anything happened to him. I found the tapes in a package just as he'd said, labeled doggie vitamins. I last saw them in the back seat of Victor's limo before this charming young maiden here blindfolded me."

"Finders keepers," the flower-child thug piped up.

"We'll see," Lilah said, casting an ominous glance at the ex-child porn star. "In any case, there's one thing I didn't find down there—that safe-deposit key he talked about at Elaine's. No key, nowhere.

"It's strange," Lilah continued. "It was when I asked him about returning the key that he began getting into his strange death trip. 'I won't need the key ever again,' he said, 'I've found the key to another kingdom.'

"I know it sounds weird. 'The key to another

kingdom.' It doesn't sound like Walter Foster. I told him it didn't. That Walter Foster is already dead, he told me, dead and born again. Come on, you and Chuck Colson, I said. But he was serious. He'd had a real spiritual conversion down there in the Caribbean, he said; not the born-again Christian sort, but something mystical. Now Walter Foster is the last person in the world I'd thought I'd hear talking like a flower child, but he was full of this hippy-dippy stuff. I just didn't know what to make of it, but he went on and on about media being 'the veil of illusion' he'd pierced through; how he'd had a vision on the other side of that veil; how the scales fell from his eyes and he saw Elaine's was a Temple of Illusionists, his table the altar piece and he, Foster, the high priest.

"It was charming in a way. Maybe it was intended with the obits in mind, but he seemed so earnest and so sincere about the 'phoniness' of it all—he was like a 50-year-old Holden Caulfield. He may have been the only completely sincere customer in all of Elaine's. It stopped being charming when he started talking about death. He kept saying something like he had to 'exorcise the karma' he had created at his table. When I asked him what he was talking about, he said he could offer himself as a sacrifice upon his altar, purge negative karma by taking it with him into his next few reincarnations.

"By this time I was getting a little nervous. I tried

to talk him out of the suicide trip. I said to him, 'Why don't you just start another magazine empire, Walter? You're not too old. You could be right back at the center of everything at Elaine's. Table and all.'

" 'No,' he said. He had to go through with his self-sacrifice. 'Don't you understand?' he told me. 'I know now that life is more than the name of a dead magazine. I don't want to become what I already was. I want to be remembered for what I've become!' It got very convoluted.

"Just before the lights went out—he kept looking at his watch so I'm sure he'd arranged an exact time for the blackout with some flunky like Victor, here—the whole rap turned biblical, and I got lost. He said something about the jawbone of an ass and the pillars of the Philistine temple and—"

"Samson!" This was Saperstein the cabalist suddenly coming out of his fog. "Samson killed heaps of Philistines with the jawbone of an ass, but then when he pulled the pillars of the Philistine temple down on top of himself *and* the Philistines, the Bible comments that 'the dead which he slew at his death were more than they which he slew in his life.' Book of Judges, chapters 15:16 and 16:30. You could look it up."

"Highly intriguing," Victor spoke up. "One could see the jawbone of the ass a metaphor for the media power he once had and, well, it certainly looked as if he wanted the pillars of Elaine's society to come tumbling down on top of his corpse. Don't forget," Victor added, "I was an English major before I became a pimp."

"Don't you see now, Inspector?" Lilah pleaded. "He thought he was performing some religious mission. When the lights went out he stood up. I knew he had the gun in his hand, and I tried to stop him. I got my hands on it once—that explains the prints—but he wrenched it around and suddenly it went off. I went into shock and just ran blindly out of the place."

When Lilah finished, everyone in the room turned their attention to Dockery.

"I guess that explains everything then, huh?" the celebrity homicide cop began blandly. "He was born again to kill himself, you were just an innocent bystander who happened to have your hand on the gun, and you must think I was born yesterday."

"But, Inspector," Lilah protested. "It's all true. It happened just like that."

"Oh, I don't doubt you for a moment, young lady. I've heard of stranger things in thirty years of celebrity murder cases, although I can't think of one offhand. It's just that with a story like that you're a cinch to be indicted. And if you try telling that story to a jury, they won't be able to keep a straight face even if you could.

"They'd probably make it Murder Two what with the blackmail motive. Fortunately for you and for the rest of the criminal element in this room, there's not going to be a trial; there's not even going to be an indictment. The case is going to be closed in twelve hours, because we're all going to participate in a little coverup. As for you, young lady, you're going to give me a cleaned-up statement, and then you're going to leave the country for a while. We're going to forget the religious bullshit, and you're just going to say he was despondent. Forget that 'struggling for the gun' story. You probably made it up anyway. We're gonna wipe your prints off the gun, and then Saperstein is gonna slip into the slab room and put some prints from the stiff on it. We'll tickle the autopsy and ballistics data, and then we're going to declare it suicide."

"But it was suicide," Lilah said. "I just told you that . . . ."

"There's a difference between you saying it and me saying it, young lady. I got to tell it to a DA and a pack of reporters. You say what I tell you to say and you walk. You don't play along and you walk out of here in cuffs. I don't give a shit about the consequences to you, but there are other kinds of consequences a man in my position has to consider."

"Inspector," Victor suggested. "Perhaps we could all participate in this little coverup with more un-feigned enthusiasm if you could be more explicit about the purpose it serves."

"Unless you have enthusiasm for kidnapping, extortion, and morals charges, you'll do exactly what I say. Besides, isn't it obvious what will happen if this turns into a full-scale murder case? Every goddamn thing The Trick wanted to come out will come out—all the secret scandal—and this time with murder mixed in.''

"Goddamn. It will be the media's own Watergate,'' I exclaimed. "Not only will it show the depravity, hyprocrisy, and moral bankruptcy of the people who drove Nixon out of office, it'll look like these media people would use murder for their coverup, not just hush money like Nixon. Walter Foster's death in Elaine's is like the 'smoking gun' in the Oval Office of the media barons. My god, it could be enough to fuel a final Nixon comeback.''

"Interesting you should mention those particular words, *final comeback*.'' This was Victor talking now. "Those words ring a bell.'' Victor lit a cigarette. "The final comeback,'' he repeated. "I heard that phrase tossed around a few times in the presence of the Colonel and his new employer, Mr. Letzgo. Apparently a number of very wealthy friends and sympathizers of the former President were talking about some sort of 'legal restoration of the legitimate presidency.' I'm not sure whether they had constitutional means in mind. This could be their Reichstag fire.''

"I must insist on pointing out,'' the Colonel said, "that my employer, a productive citizen of Costa Rica, has never attempted to meddle in U.S. politics since his, ah, phony indictment. In fact, he asked me specifically to come to New York to check on the activities of

Foster in relation to these mythical Golden Greek tapes in order to prevent any meddling."

"I don't believe a word of that, Colonel," Dockery said. "But you all must admit the consequences of *not* covering up begin to look very messy, don't they, ladies and gentlemen? You could even say national security is involved here."

I looked at Dockery closely. I just could not tell what was going on behind his grim expression.

"Maybe, Inspector, you could tell us what's in it for you?" I asked. "Aside from devotion to national security."

"Well, sonny, there's Social Security for one thing. I'm past due for retirement. The wife's got a place picked out in Orlando, not far from Disney World, and I want to use up some of my pension before my second heart attack. If we don't wrap this case up right now, I'm in for a year of wallowing in filth, and I want out now.

"Okay, enough jabbering. Let me tell you something about a coverup. The reason The Trick fucked up Watergate was that he could never bring himself to come through with the pardons that the burglars were demanding. He got them cash, plenty of cash, but they still faced doing time—35 years max. Okay. I'm the law in homicide in this town. You're all pardoned. Or better, you're on probation, because my guys will be watching you. There's another thing I can do The

Trick couldn't. Or wouldn't. I can take out a contract on each and every one of you. Now get out of here, all of you, before I get sick."

"Uh, Inspector, there is one thing we've all forgotten, isn't there? The videotapes. Lilah has hers, but there are dozens more. What has become of them, might you know?"

"Saperstein and I have a good idea where they are, but because of the danger of leaks, of course we can't tell you. But as soon as we get our hands on them, we intend to light a fire and destroy them once and for all."

. . .

There's a place called the Market Diner on West Street in Lower Manhattan down by the Hudson River, and it's maybe the best place to eat breakfast in the world. A noisy place, but soothing: the clatter, the steaming urns of astringent coffee, the clouds of hot mist from the silverware steamers, the cool stainless steel, and formica surfaces. Breakfast there for me does what hours of Zen meditation in the hot baths of Esalen do for others. Myself, I'd take it over Elaine's any day. Two hours after our escape from the Golden Greek's apartment, I was sitting in a booth with Lilah, a huge breakfast, and a couple of unanswered questions.

"Lilah," I said. "Of course I didn't want to bring

it up when the Inspector was grilling you about your relation to Foster, but you did leave out that horrible practical joke he played on you. The nervous breakdown it caused."

"What are you getting at? Why make the cop suspicious? He didn't believe me anyway. And Foster didn't know I knew he was behind that episode. You don't still think I killed him, do you?"

"Well, I just wonder if your version of Foster's death last night at Elaine's was the whole truth."

"Darling, it was the *essential* truth. That's what counts. I only made up one tiny thing."

"Which is?"

"Well, I *didn't* try to talk him out of suicide. I thought it might be the best thing. Why stop him? I thought it was a heroic gesture. It was his finest hour."

For a while I wondered what *had* happened to the Golden Greek tapes so many people wanted so badly. Had Dockery and Saperstein found and destroyed them? Or were they in the hands of the 'final comeback' group?

As I write this I no longer wonder. Dockery has retired from the force. He's got three networks bidding for a prime-time series based on his best celebrity homicide cases. He just sold the rights to his life story to a big publisher for a six-figure advance and he's got several heavyweight writers "very interested" in writing it. He sits up at Elaine's at a table reserved for him and Saperstein, wheeling and dealing. Dockery's becoming a big-time agent for other cops and cop shows—while Saperstein writes cabalistic formulas on napkins and tries, like the ancient mariner, to press his calculations upon one in three. With some success: one of the three networks has given him a fat consultant's fee to determine the "mystical significance" of the Nielsen Numbers. Saperstein seems content with that, despite lucrative offers by certain publishers for a book and TV series about an "investigative morgue man."

The talk was it took a lot of pleading and groveling by several network heavyweights before Elaine relented and granted that odd couple the right to sit at Walter Foster's old table.